Please return/renew this item by the last date shown

worcestershire
countycouncil
Libraries & Learning

D1374703

SEAFIRE

SEAFIRE

BILL KNOX

Constable • London

Constable & Robinson Ltd
3 The Lanchesters
162 Fulham Palace Road
London W6 9ER
www.constablerobinson.com

First published in Great Britain 1970
This edition published in Great Britain by Constable,
an imprint of Constable & Robinson Ltd 2010

A copy of the British Library Cataloguing in Publication
Data is available from the British Library.

UK ISBN: 978-1-84901-157-0

Printed and bound in the EU

PEFC
PEFC/16-33-111
CATG-PEFC-052
www.pefc.org

Chapter One

The girl in the white MG hardtop was second in the line nosing aboard the tiny ferryboat for Kylestrome. She used a lot of accelerator for the ramp, her brake-lights flashed on as the car bounced on to the open deck, and the two-seater stopped almost under the tail of the milk truck ahead.

Webb Carrick grinned, then took the Department's grey Ford station wagon forward as a ferryhand signalled. He switched off behind the MG, another car growled aboard to occupy the last remaining place, and the loading ramp slammed shut. The ferry's propellers began churning and they eased away from the south shore for the five-minute crossing of the Loch Cairbawn narrows.

Swaying, shuddering a little, the ferry met the first light Atlantic-born swell. It was an early spring Tuesday evening in March and the sea-loch's framing of island and mountain was a gold and black glory of sunset beauty. Scenic wonder was commonplace along the Scottish coastal highlands but the Kylestrome crossing usually offered a special reward for travellers who penetrated so far north.

Carrick yawned, placed a cigarette between his lips, then left it unlit as the MG's door opened and the girl emerged in a swing of long, slim legs clad in figure-hugging red ski-pants. She gave a thankful, animal-like stretch which told of a lot of miles behind that

1

driving wheel then briefly checked the leather straps which lashed a small suitcase to the car's luggage rack. Carrick watched appreciatively. The ski-pants were matched by a Scandinavian-style anorak, her long dark hair was topped by a perky peaked leather cap, and as she removed her heavy sunglasses and tucked them in a pocket she saw him and gave a brief, casual smile. Then she'd climbed back into the MG, the door had closed, and he was left with a memory of calm dark eyes, a slightly Roman nose and a wide mouth which had a hint of humour at the edges.

Carrick yawned again, lit the cigarette, and slouched deeper in his seat. Outside, the ferryhand went by, heading for the wheelhouse and scrupulously avoiding looking at him. But Carrick's uniform and the Fishery Protection badges on the station wagon door would have registered. When the ferry reached the north shore there would be a phone call to the next fishing harbour and from there another to the next. Fishery Protection men were the equivalent of sea-going police in Scottish coastal waters. And whether it was the slim destroyer-like lines of a fishery protection cruiser off-shore or the sighting of a solitary individual on land, the fishing villages, even the most law-abiding, kept their intelligence network primed.

Not that it mattered this time. Carrick chuckled at the thought. He'd driven a long way that day and made good time – all the way from Oban, where HM fishery cruiser *Marlin* had put in at dawn to set him ashore with his hastily packed gear.

'All set for a month's holiday,' was how *Marlin's* stubby, bearded commander had sourly described the situation. Captain James Shannon bitterly resented having to lose his chief officer, no matter for how short a period – not so much from affection as from the watch-keeping problems it created for the remainder of his current patrol.

But the signal radioed from Department headquarters at Edinburgh had been precise and final.

CHIEF OFFICER CARRICK TO IMMEDIATE TEMPORARY ACTING COMMAND RESEARCH M.F.V. CLAVELLA, LYING QUINBEGG HARBOUR. EXPEDITE TRANSFER. CAPTAIN JEFFREY, CLAVELLA, TO COMMENCE ANNUAL LEAVE ON HANDOVER.

'The *Clavella's* small enough, I suppose. And someone has to fill in.' Shannon hadn't exactly generated confidence. 'Even you can probably keep her out of trouble for four weeks if you try.'

But a bottle of Shannon's prized single-malt whisky had by some magic been lying on the rear seat of the Department station wagon when Carrick collected it for the drive north. Which was as near to good wishes as Shannon, senior captain of the Protection flotilla and coming near to retirement age, was ever likely to extend.

The ferry's propeller beat slackened, her helmsman began to ease her blunt bow up-current, ready for the final approach to the north shore slipway. The milk truck's engine started in a cloud of thick blue exhaust.

Carrick turned again to the road map lying on the passenger seat. Fifteen miles more of the A894 coast road and he'd be at Quinbegg – probably just before nightfall. Which would give him a chance to view the *Clavella* before reporting aboard.

He wanted that. A motor fishing vessel, even one crammed with scientific gear, was a fairly small start. But despite the 'temporary acting' basis she was still his first genuine independent command. And he imagined Andy Jeffrey wouldn't wait around after the

3

hand-over. Only a couple of years older than Carrick and equally unattached, Jeffrey was big, blond in the Viking mould and had a single-minded hobby interest – with a scorching series of near-escapes from matrimony to prove it. He would have a heavy programme lined up for the month ahead.

As for his own role during that month, Carrick was ready for pretty well anything. The m.f.v.'s scientists could be involved in any of a score of fisheries research projects from routine plankton counts to hydrography and the mysteries of environmental study. Quinbegg, less than thirty miles from Cape Wrath, the stormy northern tip of mainland Britain, was a base that offered plenty of scope. It had rich shallow water fishing banks off-shore, plenty of deep-water areas further out in the turbulent waters of the North Minch between the mainland and the Hebridean islands. There was no sense in trying to guess the *Clavella's* current purpose.

Murmuring in, the ferry nudged against the concrete slipway. Her bow ramp came down and Carrick started the station wagon as the milk truck rumbled ashore. The girl in the MG did the same then took off in a hurry, turning for the coast route in a series of rapid gear changes.

Following, letting the gap between them widen, Carrick had a brief glimpse of Kylestrome village before the narrow single-track road began to climb and cut inland. In a few minutes he was driving through an almost empty landscape fringed to one side by mountains and to the other by the broad width of Eddrachillis Bay – where the sea was now a sweep of that golden glitter and the sun a mere fiery tip on the horizon.

The MG still occasionally showed ahead till a mail van came trundling towards him, heading south.

4

Carrick had to pull into the nearest passing place to let it through and after that he was alone on the road.

At exactly seven fifteen by his watch, dusk already greying overhead, he reached Quinbegg and drove past the village's clustered cottages to the tiny harbour. A couple of neat, dark-hulled seine netters were tied to the old stone quay. A few smaller craft were moored within its shelter. But there was no sign of the *Clavella*, only an empty, waiting berth.

Carrick pulled up, got out, and swore softly. By all that was normal and reasonable Andy Jeffrey should have had the m.f.v. lying there, his kit already on the cobbled quayside, proposing that there was maybe just time for a quick one at the village inn before he disappeared.

But if something had happened, something enough to upset the normal and reasonable ... Carrick's mouth twisted wryly as he started walking along the quay. He had the uneasy feeling that all he was certain to find was trouble. Which, as he'd already been warned, was the one thing temporary acting commanders were wise to avoid.

The only person in sight was a thick-set fisherman in overalls and white thigh-length waders, making a leisurely job of hosing the deck of the nearest seine netter.

'Any idea when the *Clavella*'s due back?' hailed Carrick.

Hose still dribbling water, the man considered him blankly for a moment then shook his head.

Carrick sighed, walked on till he reached the end of the quay, and wondered what he should do next. A gull skimmed across the water, calling harshly. The two navigation lights at the harbour entrance were beginning to burn brightly in the grey dusk. But the sea beyond was empty, its waves lapping lazily against the quay's granite walls.

5

He turned back, cursing Andy Jeffrey.

'If you're looking for the Government boat then you've a time to wait, friend,' declared a slow, deep voice. 'She sailed from here not more than two hours ago.'

A tall, thin man stood a few yards away, his lined, unshaven face expressionless below an untidy shock of long, mousey hair. As Carrick crossed over he waited silently, a strange figure in a frayed black jacket, shabby grey trousers and heavy black boots. His once-white shirt was topped by an old-fashioned stiff collar and he had no tie. Deep-set blue eyes considered Carrick in an oddly thoughtful fashion.

'When should she be back?' asked Carrick.

The thin shoulders shrugged, the voice hardened a shade. 'When whatever evil work they're about is done. All the word Captain Jeffrey left was it would be sometime late tonight.'

'Thanks.' Carrick smiled a little. 'You sound as if he's not one of your favourite people.'

'The captain?' The gaunt, stubbled face wrinkled a faint protest. 'He wears the same uniform as you, friend, except for a little extra gold braid on the sleeves. I'd call him a likeable man with a happy approach to life.' The wrinkles deepened into a scowl. 'But he has others aboard, men who use their glass tubes and microscopes to blaspheme against nature.'

Bewildered, Carrick blinked at him. 'Meaning?'

'That they sow death on the water.' A grim forefinger beckoned. 'See for yourself.'

He led Carrick to the edge of the quay and pointed down. In the failing light dead fish floated belly-up, dull silver among the harbour flotsam. Here and there were seabirds, equally dead, their feathered carcases seeming to quiver each time a wave rippled in.

'Ask them on the *Clavella* why this has happened – here and for half a dozen miles around,' said the

6

stranger deliberately. 'Ask the fishermen in Quinbegg why their nets are empty – and why such things have only happened since those people who call themselves scientists arrived.'

Carrick pursed his lips and looked again. The fish weren't the usual discards found floating around most harbours after a catch had been sorted. Many were mature, full-grown specimens of cod and whiting. He lost count of the other varieties. But there were between eighty and a hundred dead fish and perhaps a score of seabirds either floating or cast up along the tide-line.

'It's unusual,' he admitted warily. 'But – well, I've seen worse. There can be plenty of reasons.'

'That's what we've been told.' It came with a flat disbelief. The man shrugged again. 'We'll see. But someone else is looking for Captain Jeffrey. She said she'd wait at the Corrie Arms, up in the village.'

'A girl?' Carrick raised an eyebrow. 'Driving a white sports car?'

The man nodded, thrust his long, bony hands into the pockets of the black jacket, and turned as if to leave. Then he stopped. 'Around Quinbegg I'm called Preacher. Whatever you're here for, chief officer, we'll certainly meet again. Perhaps very soon.'

Before Carrick could answer he had gone, heading along the quay towards the seine netters. Watching the strange figure for a moment Carrick shook his head then went back to the Department station wagon.

He found the Corrie Arms easily enough. It was a low, slate-roofed inn about halfway along the village main street, plenty of laughter and noise coming from behind the brightly lit windows of its public bar, the separate hotel entrance located further along with a

7

plaque to one side advising that the local Rotary Club met on Thursdays.

Webb Carrick parked at the pavement's edge, switched off, lit a fresh cigarette, and sat behind the wheel for a spell, uneasily aware that he'd arrived at the edge of a brew of potential trouble.

Wryly, he considered himself in the driving mirror and wondered exactly what he was going to have to take on. The weather-bronzed face that looked back at him from below the naval cap with its gold Fishery Protection badge was broad-boned, the lips a little too thin to allow the notion that an easy-going manner meant he could be pushed around.

Thirty-one years old, a stocky five foot ten in height with muscular shoulders, the rest of the picture was dark brown eyes, darker brown hair and what had become a faintly cynical view of life.

Most of that viewpoint had been shaped in the couple of years he'd been with Fishery Protection. Which in turn had begun when, a deep-sea merchant navy first mate, he'd passed for his master's ticket but couldn't find a ship to match. Instead, he'd been called for a Fishery Department interview on the strength of a half-forgotten application – to emerge as *Marlin's* new chief officer under Captain Shannon and with the black warrant card which announced that one Webster Carrick was an assistant Superintendent of Fisheries.

Only fishery cruiser captains rated as full Superintendents. Their powers let them act as their own judge and jury when it came to settling most disputes among the fishing fleets. But having any kind of role in Fishery Protection meant being a combination of sea-going policeman and civil servant with problems to match.

As he might have now, if the black-coated Preacher's warning and those dead fish in the harbour meant anything. Carrick grimaced at the mirror and ran a finger round the collar of the white roll-neck sweater he wore under his uniform jacket. Then he stubbed his cigarette on the dashboard ashtray and climbed out.

Right now he wanted a drink and a meal. Andy Jeffrey could explain the rest later.

He hoped.

The Corrie Arms had a lobby dominated by a couple of moth-eaten stag heads and the shirt-sleeved little man sitting half-asleep behind the reception desk looked equally glassy-eyed. But he came awake enough to announce that it would be another half hour before the dining room would open.

'I'll wait. And I might need a room later.' Carrick glanced at the register lying on the desk. 'Got one available?'

'Aye. We can manage something.'

'Good.' The register interested him. The last signature on its list was a Miss M. Atholl with an Edinburgh address and the white MG's registration number opposite it. 'Has Captain Jeffrey from the *Clavella* booked a room for tonight?'

The desk clerk nodded and thawed a little. 'That's why I said we could manage something, mister. He said he was starting his leave as soon as someone arrived to take over. Reckon that's you – and only one of you will be sleeping ashore and needing that room, right?'

'Uh-huh.' Carrick grinned. 'What about his girl-friend?'

'Her wi' the red trousers?' The sleepy face creased into a heavy wink. 'Well, as long as they're paying for the two rooms –'

9

'I always like a man of high principle,' said Carrick dryly. 'All right, I'll be in the bar till feeding-time.'

He headed along a corridor in that direction, saw a men's room, and turned in. Considerably fresher after a wash, he was drying his face on a thin, much-used towel when the corridor door swung open again.

The two fishermen who came in were burly youngsters still in work clothes, silvery scales clinging to their folded-down rubber boots. The taller, half-supported by his friend, was moderately drunk, unsteady on his feet, and fairly happy about it – till he saw Carrick's uniform. He swayed, peered and scowled.

'Hey, Tam! Here's one o' the queer fellas off that Government boat.' As the other nodded warily he took an uncertain couple of steps nearer on his own, his slurred voice rising. 'Fish res – researchin' it's called, eh? Well, we know wha' you lot are doin' all right. An' we're going to fix every last one o' you baskets. Fix you for good, understand?'

'Steady it, Danny,' warned his friend, grabbing for an arm.

But he shook clear and lurched nearer. 'What's the stuff you're usin' out there, eh?' he hiccoughed. 'I'll tell you wha' you are, Mac. You're a bunch o' – o' bloody killers, that's what. Leavin' us with nothing in the nets but dead fish an' dyin'. Well, hell mend you –'

The wild, windmill swinging blow was clumsy and overdue. Carrick brushed it aside, placed one open hand against the drunk's chest, and heaved him back into his friend's arms. The man grabbed, pinned the youngster by the arms, and this time held tightly.

'Sorry, mister,' he said awkwardly above the continued flow of angry, mumbled curses. 'He's had one too many, that's all.'

10

'One is an understatement,' said Carrick frostily, lifting his cap from a peg. 'If he goes around trying to clout people that way he could end up with a broken jaw.' He reached the doorway and paused. 'How much of what he was babbling makes sense to you?'

The fisherman swore to himself as his companion struggled again, swung round to jam him against the tiled wall, and shook his head. 'Ach, how would I know what's happenin'? He's right that the fish are dyin' an' catches aren't worth a damn. But I'm not blamin' anyone, whatever's said. Not yet.'

Carrick nodded shortly and thumbed at the now woebegone drunk. 'Try sticking his head under a tap. And keep it there.'

He went out, leaving them to argue.

The bar was warm, oak-panelled, smoke-filled and moderately busy. He reached the counter, ordered a beer, and was paying for it when a hand fell on his shoulder.

'Your name Carrick?'

He turned, nodding. The man was plump, sallow, and middle-aged, his dark hair heavily streaked with grey. He was medium height and barrel-chested beneath a baggy but expensively tailored suit of heather-hued island tweed. He had a checked wool shirt and a knitted dark blue tie.

'Captain Jeffrey told me you'd gravitate here. I'm Harvey Robertson – auxiliary coastguard. Like to join me? I've already collected someone else for him.'

Robertson gestured to a table in a far corner of the bar. The girl from the MG was there, a drink in front of her. She looked up and smiled as they came over.

'Party complete,' said Robertson briskly. His words came clipped, the accent far from home. 'Miss Atholl, this is the man we need. Mr Carrick is due to take over the *Clavella*.'

'That helps,' she said wryly. 'Now all we've got to do is wait.' She looked at him again. 'Weren't you on the ferry, just behind me?'

He grinned and nodded, took the chair Robertson offered, and sat down. 'So we're both waiting on Andy Jeffrey?'

'Correct,' agreed the girl. She grimaced good-naturedly. 'Well, I'll tell him a couple of things when he shows up. Like how I started driving from Edinburgh at dawn to get here as I'd promised –'

'He hadn't planned on sailing,' soothed Robertson defensively. 'But his research people suddenly announced conditions were ideal for something they had to do.' Sipping his glass of neat whisky, he glanced at Carrick with a touch of sympathy. 'I've pretty much the same message for you. They're tidying up the end of a project programme.'

'Any idea what they're working on?' queried Carrick.

'Me?' Robertson's heavy face crinkled with amusement. 'None at all. You could put all I know about marine biology on the back of a postcard. Even the coastguard thing I mentioned is just bad-weather volunteer duty.' He sipped the whisky again. 'No, my only claim to fame around Quinbegg is that I own the local garage. But I know the *Clavella* people and I'm here most evenings so Captain Jeffrey asked me to look out for you both – and he's the persuasive type.'

'Persuasive is the word,' murmured the girl almost to herself. Then she sat back with a sigh. 'Well, now we know. Captain Carrick –'

'Wrong rank,' corrected Carrick sadly. 'I'm only a stand-in – all I rate is chief officer's pay, which is a lot less. And my first name is Webb.'

'Mine is Mora.' She smiled across the table. 'Mr Robertson, it looks like we should both thank you for your trouble. But I'll still have a few questions for Andy Jeffrey when he does show up.'

'I've a couple of my own,' mused Carrick, his eyes straying along the busy bar counter. A cluster of fishermen, probably from the seine-net boats, were drinking near the main door. They'd been watching him but now they deliberately turned away. 'None of us expect a Fishery Protection uniform to be a passport to instant popularity but around here it seems to rate deep-freeze treatment.'

Robertson nodded warily. 'Relations between some of the fishermen and the *Clavella* people are – well, they aren't at their best. There's a damned stupid notion among the local boats –'

'That her research boys are trying to kill off most of the sea life?' Carrick saw the man's eyebrows rise and nodded in turn. 'I heard the story at the harbour, from an earnest-sounding character in a black coat.'

'Who looked like he needed a shave?' queried Mora Atholl. 'I met him too. But I didn't get any story.'

Robertson sniffed as if an unpleasant odour had been dumped under his nose. 'You met one of our local problems, Preacher Noah – the Noah part because he lives in an old boat in the harbour.' He scowled briefly. 'Someday the sanitation people will tow the thing out and sink it. When that happens, they should leave him aboard. He's the kind of loud-mouthed nuisance who'll climb on a soap-box and howl at the world any time, anywhere.'

'He seemed harmless enough.' Carrick shrugged and shifted forward in his chair. 'But I certainly got the start of a lecture about the *Clavella* being involved in some kind of nastiness. What's it all about?'

'I'd like to know too,' said the girl, frowning a little. 'Something must have been happening. Andy's leave should have started last week. Then almost at the last minute, right out of the blue, it was cancelled and we

13

both had to shuffle arrangements.' She sighed. 'Last time Andy phoned I got the feeling he was really desperate for us to get away.'

'That's possible.' Carrick said it soberly but the glint in his eyes made her redden.

Robertson grunted, oblivious to the by-play. 'All that's happened comes down to a few dead fish and birds. But from the fuss you'd think a plague had struck.'

'Beginning after the *Clavella* arrived.'

'Coincidence.' For a moment Robertson appeared almost uneasy. He emptied his glass, set it down, and sucked his teeth. 'Look, Carrick, unless you're accepting that your own people –'

'All I'm doing is expressing an interest,' soothed Carrick. 'An interest, and trying to find out what kind of mess I'm inheriting.'

'Meaning you think Andy made that mess?' asked Mora Atholl, frowning.

'He knows his job and he does it well. He also happens to be a friend,' Carrick told her. 'But it looks like his public relations have been slipping.' Thumbing towards the fishermen at the bar, he asked Robertson, 'Do most of them feel like Preacher about what's happened?'

'How would I know, damn it?' The man gave a long, unhappy sigh. 'You'd have to be born among them to be sure. I only arrived in Quinbegg a couple of years ago – up here that rates as yesterday.'

Mora showed surprise. 'People seem friendly enough.'

'That's standard-size Highland hospitality,' snapped Robertson. 'Live among them and they're friendly, polite, accommodating, all the rest of it – but that doesn't mean you know what goes on in their minds.' He stopped, glanced at his watch, and his sallow face showed relief.

'If you're ready we can probably go through and eat now. The meal goes on Captain Jeffrey's bill, part of his apologies.'

Carrick grinned. Andy Jeffrey had obviously guessed he could be returning to a fairly cool atmosphere. But it might take more than a meal to satisfy the dark-haired girl he'd left behind. Which offered certain possibilities, not the least of them connected with the memory of a plump redhead Jeffrey had once stolen the day before Carrick had been due back from patrol . . .

Humming softly, he followed them to the dining room.

The food at the Corrie Arms was simple, expensive but beautifully cooked. You forgave the small stains on the tablecloth which charted the day's breakfast and lunch, tolerated a slow-moving waitress whose notion of hygiene was to wipe the cutlery on the edge of her apron, and concentrated on the menu.

By the time they'd reached coffee via fresh loch salmon and some tender venison cuts, a programme which took considerably over an hour, Carrick knew a lot more about his companions. Harvey Robertson's garage business didn't seem to occupy much of his time. Running it was more or less left to a foreman while Robertson sold the occasional car and played around at being a country gentleman. One with a wife vaguely in the background.

'Eleanor likes Quinbegg,' said Robertson briefly. 'Maybe more than I do – but two specialists said I either quit London and came to a place like this in Scotland or I'd end up imagining I was being chased by little green men. The rat-race syndrome – next stop a complete nervous breakdown.' He held out a hand, fingers spread. 'Well, I'm steady as a rock now, I'll say that much.'

15

'And your wife?' queried Mora. 'Won't she be wondering where you are?'

'Tonight?' Robertson shook his head, a grin crossing his plump face. 'She's away for a few days, visiting some of her long-haired friends down south. And when I say long-haired I mean just that. Eleanor's the kind of woman who keeps getting involved in causes. Her idea of exercise is a protest march. Anyway, she won't be back till tomorrow, so I don't need a late pass.'

'I can understand her liking it here,' mused the girl. 'Beautiful scenery, absolute peace –'

'There's a lot of both,' agreed Robertson dryly. 'But not much else, believe me.'

Carrick nodded, but his attention was back with Mora Atholl. So far he knew she was twenty-five, single, had an appetite which was several sizes too large to go with her figure, and worked for an Edinburgh electronics outfit.

Apparently with a pretty good job when you added together the car, the expensive cut of the ski-pants and the custom-tailored simplicity of the white shirt-blouse revealed when she'd removed her anorak jacket. The blouse outlined a firm, high-peaked bust in tantalizing style each time she moved or laughed. And there was a keen mind behind those cool dark eyes. He caught himself wondering exactly why she'd come north. Andy Jeffrey's blond Viking charm could work wonders, but somehow this girl didn't match his usual pattern. There was something a little too special here, too –

She smiled at him across the table. 'You look as if you've a problem, Webb. Need any help?'

'It's something I'll work on.' He found his cigarettes while the waitress came over on slippered feet, clattered down coffee cups, then shuffled off again. 'That was a pretty good meal.'

16

'And I needed it.' She took the cigarette he offered, leaned forward to reach the flame of his lighter, and a tendril of her dark hair brushed his wrist. 'How much longer have we got, Mr Robertson?'

'Time enough for another drink after this,' declared Robertson, settling back in his chair. 'Then I'll walk down with you and –'

He broke off, frowning. The dining room door had opened. A bulky figure in police uniform stood there a moment, looked round the few occupied tables, then came straight towards them.

'For me again, sergeant?' queried Robertson with a groan. 'If it's another damned break-in at the garage –'

'Not this time, sir.' The policeman turned to Carrick, his voice quiet, his face grim. 'I'm Sergeant Mac-Kenzie, county police. Chief Officer Carrick?'

'Yes.' Carrick gestured to a chair, waited until the sergeant was seated, then asked, 'Trouble?'

'Aye, I'm afraid so.' The sergeant removed his cap, glanced at Mora, then gave an almost apologetic shrug. 'It's the *Clavella* – she's had some kind of accident aboard. No damage that I know about an' she's on her way back to harbour. But –' he stopped and rubbed an awkward forefinger along the cap's band – 'well, they've had casualties. Two dead.'

Carrick heard the girl's sharp, in-drawn breath, then Robertson's rumble of surprise. But he concentrated on the policeman.

'You've got names?'

'Aye. They were Captain Jeffrey himself and a John Humbey.' The sergeant saw the question coming and shook his head. 'That's about the lot I know, sir. The boat has been in radio contact wi' the shore, but all I got was a phone message from Fishery Protection headquarters asking me to find you.'

Face pale, Mora Atholl clumsily stubbed her cigarette in an ashtray. 'There's no chance of a mistake, sergeant?' she asked in a small, tight voice. 'About – well, about the names I mean?'

'None, miss. I'm sorry.'

Her lips pressed tight. Robertson shifted in his chair and it creaked loudly in the momentary silence.

'What the hell happened out there?' he demanded of no one in particular. 'John Humbey is senior man on the ship's research team. Humbey and Captain Jeffrey – it just doesn't make sense!' He scowled at the sergeant. 'You're sure there's no damage aboard, no one else injured?'

'That's what I've been told, Mr Robertson.' Mac-Kenzie switched his attention back to Carrick. 'I'm damned sorry about this, sir. If you need any help it'll be ready for the asking. You knew Captain Jeffrey?'

Carrick nodded.

'Aye.' It came sympathetically. 'Well, there's no rush about getting down to the harbour. The word is she won't arrive for at least another hour. I'll be there if you need me.' He cleared his throat and considered Carrick carefully for a moment. 'If you want to make radio contact wi' her just now –'

'No.' Carrick imagined things were probably bad enough aboard *Clavella* without that happening. 'But I need a telephone. Fishery Protection may have heard something more by now.'

'Use a line from the police station,' suggested Sergeant MacKenzie, glaring at the hovering, frankly gossip-gathering waitress. 'You'll have privacy there, which is more than I can say for some other places.'

'Go ahead,' invited Robertson quickly. 'I'll stay with Mora till you get back.'

'I'll be glad of the company but I'll be down at the harbour,' she said quietly, moistening her lips. 'I'd rather wait there.'

Robertson shrugged, looked surprised, but didn't argue.

18

Following the sergeant out, Carrick was glad to escape from the blend of incredulity and shock still lingering on Mora Atholl's face. Yet, strangely, somehow he had the impression of only a minimal amount of grief. Maybe she was just made that way. Suddenly Webb Carrick wished he was still back on *Marlin*, still taking orders, anywhere, except here at Quinbegg waiting for tragedy and his first command to come sailing in together.

Chapter Two

Ten minutes later, using the telephone in the charge room of Quinbegg police station, Carrick listened to the voice of Captain Prescott, duty night officer at Protection headquarters, and felt even worse.

Rasping in his ear, distorted by distance, Prescott's words kept to a tight, basic outline of the situation but still etched a cold, factual horror.

'What we've got from the *Clavella* so far is fragmentary. But Jeffrey and this boffin Humbey were crewing one of the two-man towed submersibles the research bods keep playing with. You know the things?'

'Yes.' Carrick had seen them being serviced ashore – streamlined steel porpoises maybe fifteen feet long and weighing around two tons. The two-man crew lay side-by-side, had observation windows, and could control depth and to a degree direction as if in an underwater glider. But the submersibles had no independent drive and depended on a steel trawl warp which attached them to the towing vessel. 'Where were they working, sir?'

'Roughly sixteen miles north-west of you. There's the start of a streak of deep water out there. It's called the Quinbegg Trench – as deep as you'll find anywhere in the North Minch.' Prescott's voice held a harsh gloom. 'Anyway, they're down deep and being towed quite happily by the *Clavella* when the telephone link suddenly packs in. A moment later the deck team see some kind of minor eruption in the water astern. So they winch in fast – but there's damn all on the end of the tow warp except a chunk of a shackle housing from the nose.'

'But it couldn't just fall off!' protested Carrick.

'Even I managed to work that out,' snapped Prescott. 'From the *Clavella's* report the size of the chunk recovered means the interior was flooded almost instantly. There may have been a complete breakup. They've certainly recovered both bodies, which points to it. Your job now is to get aboard the moment that m.f.v. comes in. Grill the crew. But make damned sure anyone who does know anything keeps his mouth shut afterwards. Whatever you end up thinking, play the thing to outsiders as an accident – and outsiders include the local police.'

'Meaning it could have been something else?' queried Carrick slowly.

'Meaning just obey orders,' declared Prescott grimly. 'You'll have company arriving early tomorrow morning. Under no circumstances will you take that boat out or go beyond your orders before then. Understood?'

'Yes.'

'That's it then.' A sigh came over the line and the distant receiver went down.

Carrick put the telephone down slowly, suddenly remembering that before Prescott had been transferred to headquarters, while he'd still been a protection cruiser captain, there had been a spell when Andy Jeffrey was his chief officer. Prescott had his own brand of grief. He leaned his clenched fists on the desk in front of him then heard the charge room door click open. He looked round as Sergeant MacKenzie entered.

'Anything fresh?' asked MacKenzie mildly.

'They recovered both bodies. It happened under-water,' Carrick told him shortly.

'Well, at least we're not dealing wi' locals.' Mac-Kenzie rasped a hand along his broad jaw-line and explained hastily. 'Someone else will have the job o' telling relatives. In a fishing village you can get enough o' that in the average year – and I hate it.'

Carrick nodded, took the cigarette MacKenzie offered, and shared a light. Trying to sound interested, he asked, 'On your own tonight, sergeant?'

'Aye. Total strength here is myself and two con-stables.' MacKenzie yawned a little. 'We take turns at night shift, and I've been damned unlucky this far. I started on Sunday, when there was a break-in at Robertson's garage. Last night there was a punch-up outside the Corrie Arms after closing time – and now this.' He stopped and frowned. 'You'll want those bodies taken off?'

'Yes. And held till we can make our own arrangements.'

'Right.' The county man slowly checked his tunic buttons, found his hat, and rammed it on his head. 'Time I took a walk around and eased the drunks out of sight. But stay here for a spell if you like – I'll see you at the harbour.'

'Sergeant –' Carrick spoke as the man started to leave – 'about that punch-up last night. Were any of our people involved?'

MacKenzie froze, his eyes narrowing. 'Coming now, that's an odd kind o' question.'

'It wasn't meant to be,' said Carrick neutrally. 'I came here to take over the *Clavella*. I'm making sure I know how things stand.'

'That's reasonable, I suppose.' MacKenzie nodded and relaxed. 'There has been a wee flavour of trouble lately. One o' your engine-room lads was in the middle of things last night. No arrests, but I broke it up before anyone got his head bashed in.' He chuckled a little. 'Ach, if I arrested everyone who got into a fight around Quinbegg the paperwork would be diabolic. Anyway, we've only got two cells.'

He went out, still chuckling.

Carrick's smile died once the man had gone. His mind was back on the orders from headquarters. Play it as an accident. That meant they were already certain it had been something else.

Under a night sky heavy with broken cloud, her diesel exhaust a muffled throb, HM fishery vessel *Clavella* reached Quinbegg at 23.00 hours. She came in almost wearily, the men on her deck silent and grim-faced under the quayside lights, ignoring their audience of fishermen and villagers. A final brief churning of water at the stern was followed by a low creaking as the grey hull's fenders nudged the stonework. Then her mooring ropes were ashore and secured, the wheelhouse telegraph clanged, and the diesel sobbed to a halt.

'Neatly done,' murmured Harvey Robertson, standing a little way back with Carrick and Mora Atholl. He shrugged a little deeper into the heavy coat he was wearing and glanced at the girl. 'That's it. Suppose I take you back to the hotel, then later if there's anything –'

She hesitated, unwilling to take the decision. 'Webb?'

'Go on,' he nodded. 'I'll be along.'

Like the others they'd been standing there a long time in the chill night air. Standing, saying little. An old Daimler ambulance from Harvey Robertson's garage was parked inconspicuously further along the quay. The driver was Robertson's foreman, a stockily built individual in a leather jerkin who already had the rear doors open.

'All right,' agreed Mora with something close to relief. 'I'll be in my room.'

As Robertson led her away Carrick pushed through the crowd towards the m.f.v. Broad and blunt-bowed with a tall significantly empty twin-pole gantry at the stern where the submersible would normally have been cradled, she was not much bigger than the little seine-net boats which were her neighbours.

Carrick already knew her basic details by heart – three hundred tons, ninety feet long with a 600 horse-power single screw Lister diesel and a top speed of twelve knots, what she lacked in pace she made up in manoeuvrability. A bow thrust unit and an electrically driven auxiliary propeller, the latter built into the rudder section, meant fantastic handling capability.

He knew less about the crew. *Clavella*'s normal complement under her captain was a junior officer, an engineer and eight men – plus the research team. Beyond that, he'd need to learn. From names and faces to the individuals behind them.

The m.f.v. sat high with the tide and it was only a step down to her deck. Carrick went aboard, drew quick salutes from a couple of deckhands, then a thin, anxious-faced figure in dark blue working rig came hurrying down from the wheelhouse to meet him.

'Chief Officer Carrick?' The young voice was edged with tension. 'I'm glad to see you, sir. I'm Sam Paxton, the mate.'

Carrick returned Third Officer Paxton's salute and considered him carefully. *Clavella*'s mate was in his early twenties with light brown hair, a small cornsilk attempt at a beard and blue eyes which were currently narrowed with strain.

'Where are they, Sam?' he asked quietly.

Paxton understood. 'In the after deckhouse, sir. Do you –'

'Yes. I'd better start there.' Carrick thumbed at the watchers on the quayside. 'Make sure no one else comes aboard for now.'

24

'Aye aye, sir.' Paxton spoke briefly to the nearest crewman then led the way along the deck towards the stern. As they passed a davit-slung motor dinghy a slim, middle-aged man in grey sweater and slacks stepped out from the shadows.

'This is Peter Leslie, sir – Mr Humbey's assistant on the research team,' introduced Paxton with a noticeably uneasy formality.

Leslie held out a hand. His grip was firm but momentary and he had a small, almost delicate face with dark hair and long sideburns. 'It's a bad time to say it, but welcome aboard, Carrick,' he said shortly. 'Captain Jeffrey told me you were a friend of his.'

'Yes.' Carrick saw two more men in civilian clothes standing nearby. 'You're in charge of your side now?'

'Until I'm told otherwise,' agreed Leslie.

'Then we'd better have a talk. Make it in the chart-room in five minutes.'

Leslie nodded and stepped back to let them pass. Paxton led the way again to a small deckhouse near the bulk of the main winch drum, opened the door, took a deep breath, and followed Carrick in.

The blanket-covered shapes lay on canvas stretchers under the single bulkhead light. The stretchers were damp, almost black with water, and a pool had formed between them. Drawing back the nearest blanket, Carrick winced.

Clad in a two-piece rubber skin-diving suit and the remains of a life vest, the dead man appeared aged about fifty. His bald head glinted in the light but a deep wound on his face exposed the white of the jaw-bone. The upper part of the suit had been torn away and the man's rib-cage had been smashed.

The life vest's inflation cartridge hadn't been used. Wordlessly, Carrick covered the man again and drew back the other blanket.

25

Blond hair matted across his forehead, Andy Jeffrey's broad, good-looking face seemed almost peaceful despite the characteristic foam flecks of drowning still on his lips. The half-inflated life vest over his rubber suit had been ripped down one side and there were long tears in the rubber. But his body had no apparent injuries.

'Who did you pick up first?' asked Carrick softly.

'Humbey – pretty well straight away. There must have been enough air trapped in his suit. After that –' Paxton shrugged wearily – 'well, I'd dropped marker buoys and though it was pretty dark the sea was reasonable. We kept circling using the searchlights and found one or two fragments of debris. Then after about an hour Captain Jeffrey's body surfaced.'

'Near your centre point?'

The mate nodded.

It fitted. From appearances Humbey had died quickly, maybe instantly – and the way he'd appeared on the surface pointed to a major break-up of the submersible. But with Andy Jeffrey it had been different. Somehow he'd been trapped down there, trapped as he tried to get out of that steel coffin. Triggering the life vest's inflator must have been a last, desperate attempt to gain extra buoyancy and force himself free.

And eventually it had worked. For a dead man.

Carrick lowered the blanket and turned with a degree of relief to the salvaged debris. A broken section of cork lining had torn wires and a damaged switch panel tangled round it. He pushed aside an air cylinder and a discoloured section of rubber cushion pad and pursed his lips. The last item was an emergency breathing mask with a miniature air bottle attached. The glass of the mask was smashed and the air bottle's delivery valve still closed.

Disaster had come with an overwhelming suddenness.

26

Crossing to one of the portholes he looked out towards the stern and the empty gantry poles.

'Who made the final pre-launch checks on the unit?'

'They did.' Paxton gestured towards the blankets, his mouth tightening beneath the cornsilk beard. 'That included the towing shackles – our standard drill. The men going down always made their own checks.'

'Sensible.' Carrick always worked that way himself when it came to diving gear for underwater work. 'Surface safety precautions?'

'All carried out as usual, sir,' said Paxton, as if meeting a challenge. 'I had the telephone link to the wheelhouse, our leading hand was in charge of the winch.'

Carrick didn't turn from the porthole. 'Go on.'

'Well –' Third Officer Paxton chewed his lip – 'we left harbour in late afternoon, tracked south for a spell, then headed north towards the Quinbegg Trench after dusk –'

'Why?'

Paxton shook his head. 'I'm not sure. The research people were doing sea temperature sampling and I think Captain Jeffrey wanted to let them check some results. Then – well, we reached the position he wanted. After we launched the submersible I was to stay on course, maintain a regular three knots towing speed, and await orders.'

'Did you get them?'

'No.' The mate paused awkwardly. 'At least, no firm order, sir. We were towing with about two thousand feet of trawl warp out and they were about sixty feet down. I told him the echo sounder showed deeper water ahead and he said that was what he wanted. A few minutes later he reported one hundred and eighty feet – fairly close to the bottom – then the phone link went dead. That's – that's when the winch team saw an air burst astern.'

'So you ordered an emergency winch-in,' para-phrased Carrick, turning.

'No, not straight away.' Flushed and miserable, Paxton avoided his gaze and scraped a foot along the deck. 'I kept trying the phone link. Peter Leslie came charging over yelling for a winch-in but I –' he shook his head unhappily – 'maybe I just panicked. I kept shouting down the phone link for – well, maybe a couple of minutes before I really did anything.'

'I see.' Carrick kept his voice unemotional. 'Did the winch team see any change in the tow warp's strain?'

Paxton shook his head. 'When we're running, the warp is stoppered off the winch drum. It's to avoid strain. Anyway, that length of steel cable –'

'Weighs a lot on its own. The telephone cable was married to the towing warp?' Carrick took Paxton's nod without comment. 'Where's the section of nose you recovered?'

'In the wheelhouse. Sir –' Paxton made an appeal-ing gesture with his hands – 'even if I'd ordered that winch-in straight off –'

'It wouldn't have made a damned inch of differ-ence,' said Carrick brutally. 'They'd already fallen off the end of your line. Remember that.'

'Yes, sir.' It came with a thankful relief.

'Right.' Carrick gave him a faint, encouraging nod. 'Last question for now, Sam. What do you think happened to them? Let's hear what you feel. And nobody's going to eat you if you're wrong.'

Paxton managed a faint grin then his face became serious again. 'Well, they were practically bottom-hopping down there. But if they'd hit wreckage or jammed in rock the nose shouldn't have fractured – they'd have anchored us first. Unless –' he stopped, to be prodded on by Carrick's nod – 'well, it's crazy but maybe something happened inside the thing. Some kind of an explosion.'

'That makes two of us with the same idea,' murmured Carrick. 'Have you tried it out on anyone else?'
'No.'
'Then don't.' Carrick gestured towards the door. 'We're finished here. Muster some hands and move the bodies ashore. No fuss – that can come later.'

Compact, well-equipped and with a bank of auxiliary instrument panels relating to her research role, *Clavella*'s wheelhouse smelled equally of metal polish and Department issue detergent. Carrick looked round appreciatively, laid a hand for a moment on the cold, glinting brass of the compass binnacle, then considered the equally cold grey shape of the remains of the nose section.

It was heavy and he moved it closer to the light with difficulty. The welded eyes for the towing warp's shackle were solidly intact but the damage began scant inches to the rear, a jagged, torn edge which became a knife-slash fracture. No collision he could imagine would have caused that kind of break.

Leaving the shattered chunk of metal, he entered the tiny chartroom at the rear of the wheelhouse. The ship's logbook was in the top drawer of the main cabinet. He took the book over to the chart table, switched on a small striplight above, and studied the last few entries.

Andy Jeffrey's bold handwriting sprawled across the pages, but he'd kept details to the statutory minimum. Times, positions, and a few terse sighting reports formed the bulk of information. Each sailing was baldly described as 'for research programme purposes'.

Carrick reached the final entry, took out his pen and slowly added one more.

'Command assumed 23.00 hours.'

He dated it, signed, put the logbook away, switched off the light, and returned through the wheelhouse to the tiny open bridge wing overlooking the quayside. The Daimler ambulance had backed up alongside, and the waiting crowd had edged away a little, clearing a path. Looking aft, he saw why. Carried by crewmen, the two stretchers and their blanket-covered burdens were coming ashore over the gangway.

As the first seaman stepped on to the quay and steadied himself a tall, thin figure suddenly pushed forward into the space ahead. Scarecrow-like in the glare of the harbour lamps, Preacher Noah spread his arms wide in a demand for attention.

'See this and remember.' The words rang loud, the deep, grating voice sombre. 'As ye sow, so shall ye reap. And they were warned –' his eyes came up and met Carrick's gaze as he finished with a slow, deliberate emphasis – 'warned but paid no heed!'

The stretcher party paused uncertainly and there was a murmur from the crowd around. But the black-coated figure, his purpose served, swiftly stepped back among them and slipped away. In a moment the spell was broken. The stretchers moved forward again, some of the fishermen began to help, and the rest of the crowd gradually dispersed, heading back towards the village.

Tight-lipped and angry, Carrick stayed where he was until both bodies had been placed aboard the ambulance. Then as the vehicle's doors were closed and it began to pull away he quit the wheelhouse area and went down deck. Sam Paxton was there, serious-faced, talking to a wiry little jut-jawed man in rumpled blue overalls and an old woollen cap.

Paxton stiffened at his approach but the little man gave an easy, welcoming grin.

"Evening, chief. You'll no' be needing the engine-room squad again tonight, will you?'

'Your department?' queried Carrick mildly.

'Aye, but not for want o' trying for something better.' An oily sleeve wiped along the man's nose, which didn't do either much good. 'The name's Willie Dewar. I've just been tellin' young Sam that he should have gone out an' bloody well strangled that sancti- monious vulture.'

'Preacher?' Carrick shrugged non-committally. 'It wouldn't have looked good on his record.'

Dewar grinned through a mouthful of tobacco- stained teeth. 'Ach, maybe not. Well, will you need us?'

'Not till morning.'

'Good. I can stand down my two lads,' grunted Dewar. 'I heard you're from *Marlin*. How's that black- hearted captain you've got there, Jamesy Shannon?'

'He hasn't wrecked her yet,' said Carrick, amused. Captain Shannon had a capacity for making firm friends and even firmer enemies but it could be diffi- cult to tell them apart. 'You know him?'

'From years back when we went boozin' together.' Dewar smacked his lips at the memory. 'Well, we'll be ready from dawn. It'll be a salvage trip?'

'Maybe.'

Dewar nodded wisely. 'All I ask is someone gets the baskets who did for Andy Jeffrey. An accident?' he sniffed derisively. 'Like hell it was.'

Then he had gone, easing down a narrow hatchway ladder towards his cramped, oily realm.

'I didn't say anything, sir,' declared Sam Paxton anxiously. 'But most of the crew feel the same way.'

'Then make sure they keep their mouths shut,' said Carrick bleakly. 'And get hold of Leslie – I'm ready now.'

They met in the chartroom a few moments later. Peter Leslie took the only stool, Paxton stayed by the door, and they waited expectantly while Carrick perched himself on the edge of the chart table.

'Official statements can come later,' he began bluntly. 'Right now I want information only. Was it usual for your captain and senior research officer to crew together on the submersible?'

'Anything but,' answered Leslie flatly. 'Normally it was a research responsibility and we preferred it that way.'

'Then?' Carrick raised a questioning eyebrow.

'If you're asking why it happened, I wouldn't know,' replied Leslie laconically. 'But they went down together a couple of times last week, then yesterday – and of course, tonight. Humbey was pilot and Jeffrey used the passenger couch.'

'What were they doing down there?'

'No idea.' Leslie stuck his hands in his pockets, his small-boned face expressionless. 'Look, you'd better understand the set-up on this research team. There are – were four of us. Humbey was senior, then myself and two others you haven't met, Haydock and Allison. Each with his own speciality. Humbey was our expert on plankton research and bottom life ecology. My line is thermal studies and tidal stream patterns – this stretch of coast has some pretty unique features in both. The others help in general and operate their own sideline projects. But we work in our own little mental compartments most of the time.'

'This was a night dive,' reminded Carrick patiently. 'They wanted deep water. Doesn't that suggest anything?'

Sam Paxton stirred and volunteered hopefully: 'They had the camera lights mounted.'

'Considering they took the cine camera with them that's hardly surprising,' said Leslie coldly. 'But it means nothing. They had the camera aboard almost every dive last week but didn't use it. Maybe Captain Jeffrey was hoping to get a close-up of a mermaid.'

32

The mate flushed angrily but Carrick's frown kept him silent.

'The camera equipment,' said Carrick, keeping his own temper in check by an effort. 'Come on, Leslie. You've got to have some idea.'

'At night, deep water style?' The research officer read the warning signs. 'A lot of things in the sea only happen at night. Plankton rise towards the surface, fish behave differently. But if you want a real guess, maybe they just wanted to see how much dead stuff was lying around on the bottom and didn't want too many people knowing.'

Carrick took a slow, deep breath. They'd reached it at last. 'I've seen what it's like around this harbour. Dead fish, dead birds – what's the cause, Leslie?'

'Not the *Clavella*, that's for sure.' The slim figure opposite sniffed with a delicate derision. 'We knew it was going to happen. That's the reason we based here. Ever heard of dinoflagellates?'

Carrick hesitated then shook his head.

'They're an almost microscopic form of single-cell marine life. A bloom, open sea variety, occasionally highly toxic.' Leslie glanced almost contemptuously at Sam Paxton's puzzled face. 'For Third Officer Paxton's benefit that means poisonous. Anyway –' he shifted his attention back to Carrick – 'a plankton recording survey identified a few cells of an unusual toxic variety in this sector of the North Minch last spring. It only existed for a few weeks but we worked out it should be back in considerable strength by early March of this year. We were on target – it arrived a week after we did.'

'And that's the killer?' asked Carrick quietly.

'Correct,' agreed Leslie calmly. 'It works through the old ladder pattern. Shellfish and some other small life feed on the dinoflagellates. Then something bigger comes along and feeds on them, and so on – with the concentration of toxin increasing all the time. At the finish you get major concentrations in certain fish and in sea-feeding birds like shags and terns. And they die from poisoning.'

'Any risk to people?'

'Not yet and I'd say there won't be. The toxic level is too low to affect the human system – so far.'

'Just fine.' Carrick swore under his breath. 'Why didn't anyone think of telling this to the fishing crews?'

'Orders from the top,' answered Leslie shortly. He pointed a sudden forefinger. 'And it made sense, Carrick. Right now a few trouble-making idiots like Preacher Noah may think we're a boatload of baddies spreading rat-poison or worse on this part of the North Minch. But if the real situation was announced officially, if newspapers got hold of it? Whatever we said – that it was a small area, that there was no danger, that catches were sorted – people would still panic. West coast fish sales would slump overnight, and stay that way for months. The boats might as well tie up for a season and their crews sign on for unemployment relief.'

It made unhappy sense. Carrick remembered the corned beef scare that had followed an isolated outbreak in the north, and other similar situations. He rubbed a weary hand along his chin.

'Did you know any of this, Sam?'

Third Officer Paxton shook his head in embarrassed fashion.

'We kept it that way,' said Leslie, smirking a little. 'Only Captain Jeffrey knew.' He rose from his stool. 'Anything more for now? It's been a long day.'

Carrick glanced at his watch, saw with some surprise it was almost midnight, and shook his head. The research officer murmured a polite goodnight and left them.

'Need me, sir?' asked Paxton after a long silence.

'Only for a moment.' Carrick lit a cigarette and drew thankfully on the smoke. 'My gear is still ashore –' he saw the offer forming on the mate's lips – 'no, I'll get it myself. There's something else I want to do at the same time. Then I'll be back.' He paused, took another thoughtful draw on the cigarette, then added, 'Sam, I want a deck guard for the rest of the night. Two men each watch, two-hour watches. I've to be called if there's as much as a sniff of trouble.'

Paxton frowned and scraped a finger through his lightweight beard. 'You're expecting some, sir?'

'No, I'm just the nervous type,' said Carrick dryly.

He left the youngster and used the aft companion-way's narrow steps to get below. As usual on a motor fishing vessel the captain's cabin was located almost immediately under the wheelhouse. It was small and cramped with the usual spartan built-in cupboards; a repeater compass and bridge intercom were installed above the bunk, and a roll pendulum occupied the opposite bulkhead.

Old hands at the game claimed that the main benefit was a skipper who could come awake and immediately realize his impending doom. But an m.f.v. skipper's cabin still held one item of pure command luxury – the only private shower and toilet compartment aboard, squeezed into a cupboard-like space located next to the diesel exhaust trunking.

With a sense of relief Carrick looked around and saw that Andy Jeffrey had been more or less packed and ready. The bunk bedding had been changed. Two open suitcases lay on top of it, one packed and full, the other with some space remaining. The jacket and slacks the *Clavella*'s captain had intended to wear were hanging on a peg, a few other items were lying on the dressing chest.

With a strange, vaguely unreal feeling Carrick carefully gathered the dead man's belongings together and packed them in the second suitcase. He hesitated over a leather wallet and a small gun-metal cigarette lighter with the Fishery Protection anchor and laurel wreath crest etched on one side but finally added the wallet to the case and slipped the lighter into his pocket. Then he closed the suitcases, shoved them into the bottom of the cabin wardrobe, took a last look around, and went out.

Two seamen were already on duty by the gangway as he went ashore. The quayside was silent, empty, and now in darkness except for the navigation lights at the harbour entrance. But lights from the village glinted on the water as he walked along – enough for him to see as well as hear the feebly splashing shape newly grounded on the pebbled shallows.

A great, silvered cod was struggling in its death throes. One more victim for the dinoflagellates. He swore, looked away, and hurried on.

The hour might be midnight but the Corrie Arms was still very much in business. A mild gesture towards Scottish liquor licensing laws ensured the lights in the public bar had gone out, but that meant little unless you were a stranger.

At the reception desk the same shirt-sleeved clerk looked more like a sleepy-eyed dormouse than ever. He made no comment, gave Mora Atholl's room number on the upper floor, and retired straight away behind a book.

Carrick went up, tapped lightly on the girl's door, and it opened immediately. She was alone, still in blouse and slacks, and despite a repair job to her eye make-up the signs were there had been tears earlier.

'Thanks for coming.' Quietly, she beckoned him in. Her case was opened on the bed, a brief nylon night-dress had been tossed carelessly over the pillow.

Closing the door again, she said in a tired voice, 'If you'd like a drink, I could phone down.'

Carrick shook his head. 'I'm due back on board.'

A sound which might have been relief came from her lips. She waved towards the room's only chair then sat on the bed, her hands clasped over updrawn knees.

'You know what happened now?' she asked.

'Most of it.' Carrick took the chair and laid his cap beside it. 'The story is pretty much what I had before. Something went wrong with their diving unit and –'

'And he drowned.' Her fingers tightened a little. 'Indestructible Andy – that's the way I thought of him.'

'That's the way most people did.' Carrick hesitated. 'How well did you know him, Mora?'

'Meaning did we have a real thing going?' Slowly, she shook her head. 'No, I liked him but we weren't – well, you know what he was like. So did I. I met him last summer and I'd seen him a few times since. Joining him here then touring around for a week seemed a good idea. Nothing more.'

He nodded absently, glad that part was over. 'You'll go back home now?'

'I thought of that, but maybe I should stay.' Her slim shoulders shaped a shrug. 'I had an offer from Harvey Robertson before he left. His wife gets back tomorrow and they've a spare room.'

'That's pretty decent.'

'If his wife does get back.' A wry, momentary humour showed in her dark eyes. 'I'll wait and see.' The humour died away. 'Andy had relatives –'

'The nearest I know about is a brother in Canada. He'll be told.' Carrick reached into his pocket, brought out the cigarette lighter, fingered it, then leaned forward and laid it beside her. 'I found this in his cabin. I thought you might like it. As – well –'

37

Mora Atholl nodded, stayed silent for a moment, touched the crest on the lighter briefly, then asked, 'What will you do, Webb?'

'Probably begin salvaging that submersible in the morning to find out what went wrong,' he said neutrally. 'After that the Department will almost certainly want the *Clavella* to resume routine work.'

She gazed at him soberly. 'What did go wrong, Webb? Was it really an accident? Since I got here I've heard enough to – well, to know there was trouble around.'

He shook his head. 'That's one I can't answer yet, Mora.' Collecting his cap, he got to his feet.

'You have. Enough for me, at any rate.' She rose and went with him to the door. 'I think I'll stay, for a little while anyway.'

'Mind if I look in sometime tomorrow?' he asked.

'I'd mind a lot more if you didn't.' She said it quietly, and sounded as if she meant it.

Mora Atholl closed the door once he'd gone, walked slowly to the bed, lifted the gun-metal lighter, considered it silently for a moment, then put it in her suitcase and firmly closed the lid. Turning away, she began to undress.

If she had to start crying again she wanted to be in bed first, with the lights out.

The Department station wagon was still lying outside the hotel. Carrick climbed aboard, lit a cigarette, then started the engine, switched on the headlamps, and set the vehicle moving.

The road was empty of traffic on the short distance to the harbour. As he reached it Carrick slowed and turned left, planning to park on the waste ground near the quayside area. The twin beams of his headlamps swept the rough, pebbled surface.

To show in brief, sharp silhouette two startled, crouching figures who'd been dragging a man towards the edge of the harbour wall – a man who hung limp and sack-like, held by the heels, head and shoulders being pulled along the ground.

Swearing, the cigarette still between his lips, Carrick spun the wheel again, brought the headlamps back on target, and slammed his foot on the accelerator. The station wagon's engine bellowed and the vehicle lurched off the road, bouncing towards the men.

For a moment they seemed hypnotized by the glaring lights and the charging shape. Faces which registered as strange brown blobs stared as if frozen. Then they dropped their burden and began running.

Carrick braked to a halt beside their abandoned victim, saw them vanish among a maze of piled fish boxes ahead, and jumped out. Grim-faced, he knelt beside the unconscious man on the ground and swore again . . . but softly this time.

It was Preacher Noah. Dirt and blood matted the long thick hair and smeared the unshaven face and black jacket. The side-glow of the headlamps showed a long, shallow cut in his scalp. Gripping him under the arms, Carrick eased him upright a little and propped him by the shoulders against one of the front wheels then looked around.

There was a water stand-pipe a few yards away. Going over, Carrick filled his cap from the tap, came back, and splashed some of the contents over Preacher's face. He heard a moan and used the rest the same way. The thin face twisted, there was another, longer moan, the head moved, and finally the man's eyes opened and he stared up.

'You!' Recognition came with a hoarse, harsh surprise. Preacher closed his eyes again, groaned, and after a moment brought a hand up to explore the gash on his head. When he looked up there was a note of complaint in his voice. 'There's water on me.'

'You're lucky you're not floating in the stuff,' Carrick told him coldly. 'When I arrived you were on your way into the harbour. Maybe that wouldn't have been such a bad idea.' Standing back, he shook the last of the water from his cap. 'What happened?'

'Two men – from behind me.' Grunting painfully, Preacher Noah managed to haul himself to a shaky, upright position by holding on to the station wagon. 'I – I heard some sound and turned. Two of them, with faces like devils . . .'

'Forget the Old Testament stuff. They had nylon stocking masks,' said Carrick bluntly. He looked around. The harbour seemed deserted again. 'Get in. I'll drive you to a doctor – or to the police.'

'No.' Preacher tried to stand upright on his own, staggered, and grabbed the station wagon's roof for support. 'I want nothing like that – nothing. I mean it. From here to my boat isn't far. If – if you'll give me a minute –'

Carrick sighed and gave a reluctant nod. 'Come on, then. You show me where.'

Putting a steadying arm round the tall, surprisingly light figure, he started them moving. Preacher guiding, gradually becoming steadier on his feet, they headed away from the harbour wall then swung to an outer basin on the far side of the main quay. About a dozen small boats were moored around its rim. Preacher stopped.

'That one.' He pointed at an old converted lifeboat just below. 'I'll manage the rest, chief officer. And –' his lips tightened – 'yes, I owe you a debt.'

'Forget it,' said Carrick curtly.

'I tell you what I will forget.' The deep-set eyes glittered in the night gloom. 'One of these men spoke as he hit me. I heard him clearly. He said, "This is for Andy Jeffrey."'

Carrick swallowed. 'You're sure?'

'Would I say it otherwise?' Turning, still moving painfully, Preacher put his feet on the top rungs of an iron ladder and climbed down to the lifeboat's deck. Then he looked up, his deep voice strangely perturbed. 'Chief officer, I felt no joy that these men died. But I tried to use their death as a warning.'

'You made a good job of that,' grated Carrick.

Preacher shrugged sadly. 'A wise man heeds a warning.'

Ducking his injured head low, he entered the lifeboat's home-made cabin.

Five minutes later Carrick returned aboard *Clavella*, dropped his heavy canvas bag on deck, and acknowledged the salute of the seaman at the gangway.

'All quiet?'

'So far, sir.' The sailor had a Liverpool accent, cold feet, and the hope that Carrick wouldn't notice he was alone. His mate was in the galley, organizing a quick brew of tea and a fry of bacon and bread.

Carrick did notice, guessed why, and ignored it.

'Anyone gone ashore?'

'Only one of the research ba—' the seaman swallowed on it – 'officers, sir. Mr Leslie. He came back just ahead of you.'

'How long was he gone?' asked Carrick casually.

'Not sure, sir.' The seaman moistened his lips. Any moment his mate might come blundering along with that food and there would be hell to pay. 'Maybe twenty minutes or a little more.'

'It doesn't matter.'

Peter Leslie – Carrick knew surprise. If there was any connection between Leslie and what had happened he didn't know how it made sense. Almost cynically calm, unemotionally detached, Leslie was the one man who so far hadn't raised a single question about the way disaster had struck the submersible. Which was just as strange in its own way.

Yet if Preacher Noah had been dropped into that harbour, to drown or suffocate in the mud at its edge . . .

Most of Quinbegg would remember what Preacher had said earlier that night. Remember and react.

'I'll be in my cabin,' said Carrick wearily. He picked up the canvas grip and headed along the deck. He had had enough for one night.

Chapter Three

Dawn was at 7.30 a.m. The sun rose bright in the hills behind Quinbegg then climbed into a sky still cloud-laced by a gusting westerly wind. Lumpy, white-capped waves were breaking along the harbour wall, occasional spray carrying over to damp and glisten the slate roofs on the nearest cottages.

And the harbour scene had changed. Arriving singly before first light, almost a score more fishing boats from drifters to seine netters were moored in clusters along the quayside.

Webb Carrick woke to the clatter of pulley-blocks and the shouts of loaders as the first boxes of gutted and iced fish began swinging ashore to the already waiting trucks. Rubbing the sleep from his eyes, he yawned over to a porthole, looked out at the scene, then gazed beyond and had his first real view of the area.

Quinbegg sat midway along the inner curve of a horn of rocky bay, its cottages backed by rough green slopes of gorse and bracken and the darker clumpings of a promised summer heather. The charts might show the other side of the horn as a coastal maze of small islets and shoal rock. But here there was shelter. Quinbegg Bay formed as good a natural harbour location as he'd known.

Washed and dressed, Carrick had breakfast in the tiny wardroom with only a fat, tired-eyed cook-steward for company. Then, as he was leaving, Peter Leslie's two assistants on the research team arrived and introduced themselves with a cautious friendliness. The taller, Jim Haydock, was in his late twenties and walked with a limp. Matt Allison was slightly older and wore spectacles. Gauging them as a quietly reasonable pair, Carrick promised another meeting later, and went on deck.

The fish boxes were still swinging ashore. He leaned on the rail, enjoying the scene, listening to the voices, smiling at the occasional curse. But the smile faded at the edges as he saw a familiar blue-uniformed figure approach.

Sergeant MacKenzie came ponderously down the gangway, nodded a greeting, joined him at the rail, and spent a few moments silently thumbing tobacco into the bowl of an aluminium-stemmed pipe. Finished, leaving the pipe unlit, he cleared his throat hopefully.

'I'll have my own report to make today about last night's drownings, chief officer. Anything I should know about yet?'

Carrick shook his head. 'We won't get anywhere that matters till the diving unit is salvaged.'

'Aye.' MacKenzie eyed him shrewdly, found his matches, struck one between shielding hands, and puffed till the pipe was going to his satisfaction. 'I was thinking you'll need post mortem reports too. Will your folk arrange that?'

'Today.'

'That's what I expected. You'll want all the information you can.' The pipe stem pointed almost lazily towards the bustle around the boats. 'Some folk have their own theory about it already, of course. That it was a – well, a retribution.'

'And no prizes for guessing where that one came from,' said Carrick, unruffled. 'Preacher Noah can keep on complaining. But that's a pretty good load of fish coming ashore.'

'These boats went a fair way to get it,' frowned MacKenzie. 'Right over to the far side of the Minch.' He saw Carrick's raised eyebrow and nodded. 'Ach, there's hardly a boat still netting around here. It wouldn't be worth their while as things stand. And that's another reason I came along. You could have a wee spot of trouble later today.'

'More than we've got?' Carrick sighed. 'What kind this time?'

'Some o' the skippers are having a meeting. About this boat and what it's doing.' MacKenzie levered himself off the rail. 'That's all I've heard. But if there's more I'll get word to you.'

'Any warnings welcomed,' said Carrick gloomily.

He watched the policeman leave, saw some of the *Clavella*'s hands beginning a variety of deck chores aft with Sam Paxton supervising, gave a faint smile at the young mate's earnestness, and was going to join him when he saw Peter Leslie. The research officer had been coming along the quayside from the direction of the village. When he saw Carrick he hesitated in mid-stride then stiffened a little and came on.

'You're out and around early,' said Carrick dryly as Leslie reached the deck. 'Important business?'

'No. I – I went to buy some cigarettes. I don't smoke the regular brand we've got aboard.' Leslie pursed his thin lips, and thrust his hands deep into the pockets of the heavily quilted blue yachting anorak he was wearing. Carrick knew the kind. They were kapok padded, intended to give a degree of life-vest style flotation to the wearer if he fell overboard. 'Maybe it's as well I did, Carrick. I heard that the fishing skippers –'

'Are holding a meeting about us?' Carrick cut him

45

short and nodded. 'I know. Where did you get the story?'

'At the post office.' Leslie shrugged a little. 'I made a phone call to our Research Director, to his home. I wanted to keep him in the picture.'

'He'd be grateful,' said Carrick dryly. 'Was that why you went ashore last night – another phone call?'

Leslie scowled and didn't answer. He moved as if to go past and Carrick casually shifted to block his way.

'Another phone call?' asked Carrick again, more softly.

'No.' Leslie grated the word out. 'All I did was take a walk, out along the shore and back. I felt like walking. Satisfied?'

'Of course,' murmured Carrick. 'Why not? I'm just being early morning sociable.'

He eased aside to let Leslie pass. But the research officer stayed where he was, frowning in a new way, looking beyond him and upward.

Carrick turned. Still distant, little more than a speck, a helicopter was coming in low over the water from the south-west. As he watched, he heard the first murmur of its engine-beat.

'It's coming here,' said Leslie, puzzled.

'That's right,' said Carrick. And tried to keep the uneasiness from his voice. Now he knew what Protection headquarters had meant by 'company' arriving. Pretty soon it would be his turn to answer questions.

The big Westland helicopter thrashed its way across the bay with the sun on its gleaming metal hull, skirted the edge of the harbour, then settled in a miniature self-made dust-cloud on the waste ground beyond the quay. As its rotors ticked to a standstill the

46

dust-cloud settled – and with it the curiosity which had stopped work around the fishing boats.

The rhythm of unloading began again. A couple of minutes passed then the figure Carrick had expected came striding across *Clavella*'s gangway.

Commander Dobie was a small, brisk man. His uniform was a dark lounge suit, high polished shoes and a stiff white collar. He ranked as Chief Superintendent of Fisheries – and also happened to have commanded a Far East torpedo boat flotilla in World War Two, when he'd earned a double DSO. Now, however, he kept his torpedoes in a briefcase. But they could be almost as lethal.

"Morning, sir.' Carrick performed the expected salute, trying at the same time to take a final glance around the deck. Everything seemed more or less in order and Sam Paxton had swept his work detail into a new frenzy of activity at the stern.

"Morning.' Commander Dobie gave the nod of a man who had seen dawn rise at first hand and hadn't been impressed. 'Got yourself a mess of trouble this time, Carrick.' As he spoke, his eyes flickered around the motor fishing vessel. Apparently with reasonable results. A quick, gnomish smile came and went. 'I need breakfast and a couple of your men. In that order. Send the men over to that damned egg-beater. There's equipment aboard you're going to need and Clapper Bell won't enjoy moving it alone.'

'He's with you?' Carrick's surprise was genuine. Petty Officer William 'Clapper' Bell was *Marlin*'s bo'sun and his regular diving partner when it came to scuba work. But the fishery cruiser was a long way to the south – or should have been.

'Picked him up as I came,' said Dobie casually. 'What about that breakfast?'

Carrick led the way.

The galley produced a double ration of bacon and eggs in record time and, settled in front of them, eating happily, Commander Dobie listened while Carrick talked. Occasionally he'd point his fork and fire a question. But at last he seemed satisfied in terms of both fact and food.

'First we get our priorities right.' Settling back, he took out a thin, battered silver cigarette case, opened it, and lit one. 'You're ready to sail?'

'Yes, sir.'

'Good. But we'll leave that for a little.' Dobie let a puff of smoke drift up towards the ceiling of the wardroom. 'Once we do – well, if those marker buoys are in position it shouldn't be too hard to locate the submersible. Right?'

'She's lying about two hundred feet down and we'll be using regular aqualung gear.' Carrick had been turning this over in his mind for some time. 'We can do it, sir. But it's right on the limit for compressed air work.'

'That's what Clapper Bell said.' Dobie frowned for a moment. 'Carrick, this is one salvage job that mustn't go wrong. You understand?'

'I'd like to, sir.' Carrick paused fractionally and deliberately added, 'More than I do now, at any rate.'

'Fair enough.' Dobie permitted himself a thin chuckle. 'We get the thing up, we send it south by road for the experts to examine.' His voice hardened. 'I'll bet a year's pay that their report will be sabotage – sabotage and murder. You knew Andy Jeffrey. He was no fool, not during working hours at any rate. Agreed?'

Carrick nodded, waiting.

For long seconds Commander Dobie stayed silent, his eyes fixed on a calendar fixed to the bulkhead opposite. It featured a blonde pin-up girl. Someone had given her a pencilled moustache. Suddenly, he broke the silence.

'Ten days ago I had a confidential signal from Jeffrey that there had been an apparent attempt to sabotage the ship's research project. Then two days later another saying he'd struck something a whole lot bigger than he'd expected. But he insisted he didn't want outside help, that any interference could wreck his chances of finding out what was going on.'

Carrick pursed his lips in a silent whistle. 'Did he give details?'

Grimly, Dobie shook his head. 'I wanted them. But he said he'd make it a personal report, backed by evidence. Humbey knew about it and they were working together – but no one else.' His fingers drummed the wardroom table for a moment. 'He should have gone on leave last week. But I agreed to postpone it for a few days, to give him more time. Then he'd quit the ship as if starting that leave – and come straight to headquarters instead. That's why you got such a short-notice transfer. His last signal said he was almost finished, that we could go ahead with arrangements.'

Carrick stared at him. 'But he had a girl meeting him –'

'Mora Atholl. I know.' Dobie shrugged. 'He kept that going – reckoned it would make good camouflage, and said she'd play along.'

'And all because of a fishery research programme?' Carrick looked at the impassive face opposite him, felt a growing anger, and abandoned protocol. 'Commander, you sat there and nodded between mouthfuls while I talked about dead fish, dead birds and those damned dinoflagellates. You made apologetic noises when I told you how the fishermen have reacted.' He saw the little man's gathering frown but kept on. 'Now suddenly you're saying Andy and Humbey were killed because of those same water-bugs. Maybe you don't know what Andy found out. But you do know more about the research job. And I want to hear it.'

'Finished, mister?' asked Dobie dryly.

Tight-lipped, Carrick nodded.

'Good. I was going to tell you anyway.' Dobie opened his briefcase, glanced at a file inside without taking it clear of the leather, and nodded briskly. 'Had to check a name first. To start with, you know that dinoflagellates are single-cell, plant-like, multiply like fury – and are as poisonous as hell?'

'All I need to do is look across the harbour.'

Dobie was unruffled. 'You've had your growl, Carrick. Now stay quiet and listen. These things are almost unknown around the North Atlantic coastlines – they belong to the Pacific. Laddie, when you've seen them in the Pacific you don't forget it. The whole sea can be streaked red, as if it was on fire. Millions of them, tiny, deadly killers – and they work just like some kind of seafire, burning the liver and guts out of everything that absorbs them.'

'You've seen them there?' asked Carrick quietly.

'Once.' Dobie paused, eyes far away for a moment, drawing on a memory. 'That was a long time ago. But when it does happen here – well, a few years ago a type called *Gonyaulax tamarensis* turned up on the north-east coast of England from God knows where and began multiplying. Within a week we'd reports of marine life dying. Within a month hospitals had almost one hundred cases of serious paralytic shellfish poisoning – and if you want to know how bad, that toxic hits the human nervous system like strychnine. Then the dinoflagellates just faded away again. And *Gonyaulax* hasn't come back since. The stuff off Quinbegg is a different variety.'

'Worse?'

'No. I mean –' Dobie scowled – 'blast you, don't interrupt. I'm doing my best. The things here are apparently less toxic in natural concentration and so far no one's seen that seafire effect, just the results. Last spring the few there were came and disappeared again within weeks and with luck the same thing will happen this time. But last spring the research boffins collected enough of them to be able to play around with the results under laboratory conditions. For a spell, anyway. Then –' he took a deep breath – 'then we dropped the Official Secrets Act on their heads.'

Suddenly aware of the smouldering cigarette between his fingers, Dobie stubbed it out with maddening care and lit another from the silver case.

'With me so far, mister?' he asked softly.

'Toxin.' Carrick took a deep, resigned breath. 'Biological warfare. I thought we resigned from that league.'

'Nobody resigns from collecting know-how,' rasped Commander Dobie. 'Carrick, for some reason the water temperature, salinity and everything else around here alters this particular dinoflagellate for the short time it exists. Before John Humbey came on this trip with Jeffrey they were security vetted back to the day they were born. Then Humbey had a special briefing from the micro-biological specialists at Porton Down. Because they're scared of what they call Project Seafire. Scared of the kind of hell's brew essence you can culture from it. Now do you understand, mister?'

Silently, Carrick nodded. It made a difference, a very great difference. He wondered just how deep and how fast a security vetting had been run on him for Dobie to be able to open up so much.

'How are we playing it, sir?' he asked, forcing his voice to stay steady. 'Still on our own, or –'

'On our own,' rasped Dobie. 'While we can, anyway. But once the post mortem examination reports

are through and we've got the verdict on the submersible then everyone will want in on the act. That
means we've maybe a couple of days.'

'Which isn't long,' said Carrick doubtfully.

'No.' Dobie considered him carefully. 'I could have
Captain Shannon here with *Marlin* by tonight. But the
less fuss we have to make . . .' He let the rest of it die.
'Carrick, I'm going to use the wardroom as an office
for a spell. I'll start on statements from witnesses,
beginning with Third Officer Paxton. And I'll pay
particular attention to your friend Leslie. Now, is
there anyone ashore you could talk to – talk to very
casually – about Andy Jeffrey's movements when he
was in the village?'

'There's Robertson,' said Carrick. 'The garage
owner I told you about.'

'Yes.' Dobie nodded. 'And a garage is a good place
for gossip. Try him on this skippers' meeting while
you're at it. I'd like a hint of what's in the wind.'

Rising, Carrick grimaced. 'Whatever it is, Preacher
Noah will be doing the huffing and puffing in the
background.'

'He sounds a problem,' mused Dobie. 'And I've
heard of him before. I don't remember it exactly but
there was money involved, quite a lot of money.'

'He looks more like a welfare case,' said Carrick.

'When there's real money they usually do.' Dobie
laid a hand on the coffee pot and sighed. 'Gone cold.
No –' he forestalled Carrick's offer – 'never mind. It
tasted bad enough warm.' He glanced at his wrist-
watch. 'On your way, mister. But don't be too long. I'd
like you to sail at 11.00 hours. We're going to need
plenty of time out there.'

Petty Officer William 'Clapper' Bell, six feet of
bulkily muscular Glasgow-Irishman, said it more
forcefully a couple of minutes later.

52

'Two hundred feet down an' only somebody's hopeful idea of a buoy marker as a guide?' His voice boomed in protest. 'Hell's fire – does he think we're flamin' magicians?'

'Pipe down or he'll hear you,' advised Carrick with a twinkle of amusement. He thumbed towards the stacked equipment the bo'sun had arranged along deck. 'You've double-checked we've got everything?'

'Treble,' grunted Bell. 'All right if I use that deck-house, sir?'

Carrick followed his glance, mouth tightening a little. The aft deckhouse – well, it was empty now. He nodded. 'Get the stuff stowed. If you need anything, ask the mate.'

'I've seen him.' Bell sniffed a little. Rank differences had gone overboard a long time past between them. When you were diving partners that was inevitable. 'What's the kid like, sir?'

'Keen.' Carrick said it dryly. 'But he flusters.'

'Great.' Bell scratched his close-cropped fair hair with a bear-paw hand. 'I should have stayed where I was.'

'That makes two of us,' agreed Carrick. 'What happened anyway, Clapper?'

Bell shrugged. 'Ach, I was snug in my pit aboard *Marlin* dreamin' I'd inherited a distillery. Then the Old Man kicked me awake an' told me to get the scuba gear ready. We rendezvoused wi' the helicopter at ruddy dawn near the north end o' Mull. And here I am.' He eyed the m.f.v. with something close to disgust, then glanced hopefully towards the village. 'When do we sail, sir?'

'At eleven hundred.' Carrick guessed the rest. 'That gives you time for a couple of pints. Try the bar at the Corrie Arms, but don't expect the natives to be friendly.'

Bell winked. 'If I'm buyin' –'

'It might help. Anyway, keep your ears open. Particularly if a character called Preacher Noah is mentioned. But get that gear stowed before you vanish.'

Beaming, the bo'sun set to work.

The last of the fish boxes were still coming ashore as Carrick went along the quayside and for a change some of the faces which turned in his direction were almost friendly. The thought of the share-money to come was brightening many a fisherman's day.

He nodded to a couple of skippers he recognized from past encounters of the Minch, headed on, then deliberately strolled round towards the outer basin. The same collection of small craft were moored there but the cabin door on Preacher's battered lifeboat was closed and the only sign of possible life aboard was a trace of smoke curling from a small stove-pipe.

Carrick hesitated then turned away. Robertson had to come first. Retracing his steps, he reached the Department station wagon, climbed aboard, and set it moving.

Harvey Robertson's garage was at the north end of the village. It had a line of fuel pumps outside a small flat-roofed showroom then a considerably larger workshop building to the rear. Stopping the station wagon clear of the pumps Carrick left it, shook his head with a smile as a girl in attendant's overalls came over, and went past her towards the workshop area.

Inside the building a couple of mechanics were stripping down a tractor engine. They directed him over to a small partitioned office in one corner.

A light burned inside and he saw Robertson through a window-hatch. The garage owner was at his desk. Opposite him stood the stocky figure of his foreman still in the leather jerkin he'd worn when ambulance driving.

Carrick knocked on the door, opened it, and went in.

'Well, good morning!' Harvey Robertson's beefy, sallow face split in a smile. 'I was planning on coming down to see you, Carrick. Need help with anything?'

'I've a station wagon outside. The brakes could stand adjusting – if you've a man to spare.'

'The best.' Robertson glanced at his foreman. 'Take a look at them, Kip. See what you can do.'

'Keys?' asked the foreman.

'Still in the ignition.' Carrick found himself waved into a chair while the man left. Robertson beamed across the desk at him, pushed forward a cigarette box, then offered a light from a kitchen match he struck neatly between finger and thumb.

'Anything else we can do?' queried Robertson.

'Not right now.' Carrick shook his head then drew on the cigarette. 'Unless you've heard from Mora.'

'She phoned not long ago.' Robertson wasn't smoking. But he produced a stick of gum, removed the wrapper, and began chewing. 'My wife is due back at noon. We'll pick her up together – you know she's going to stay with us for a few days?'

'She said she might.' Carrick shrugged casually. 'Though I wouldn't have blamed her if she'd wanted to get right away from here.'

'To forget about it?' Robertson shook his head. 'It's better this way. Gives her a chance to work it out of her system.' He leaned forward, his manner more confidential. 'I heard some of your people came in by helicopter.'

Carrick nodded. 'The start of the usual investigation business. It . . . yes, it could involve you. Captain Jeffrey's last messages.'

'Formal stuff?' Robertson shrugged. 'Any time. But first you'll try to salvage the submersible, eh?'

'If we can.' Carrick regarded him thoughtfully. 'How well did you know him?'

'The captain?' Robertson considered for a moment, chewing. 'The *Clavella*'s been here about a month, he was in the Corrie Arms for a drink most nights and we talked – you know how it is. Then he came out to my place for a meal a few times. But that's about all.'

A pair of powerful binoculars were lying on a filing cabinet behind the desk. Carrick nodded at them. 'Did he ever ask your advice about the area? As a coastguard auxiliary, I mean . . .'

Robertson chuckled at the notion. 'Once and once only. He was keen to learn more about the fishing marks around here. I told him he'd the wrong man. When I bought this business I inherited the coastguard thing from the last owner. All it amounts to is manning a lookout point in rough weather and laying on transport for a beach rescue party when they're needed.'

'Has it happened?'

'Beach rescue here?' Robertson nodded easily. 'A couple of times last year, but no high drama stuff. We had a fishing boat run aground – the crew were drunk. Then a coaster strayed in fog and rammed some rocks.' He dismissed the memory with a gesture. 'No, I told Captain Jeffrey the man he wanted was Preacher Noah. Though whether that long-haired windbag would tell him anything is a different matter.'

'Why Preacher?' asked Carrick, puzzled.

'Didn't I tell you last night?' Robertson blinked apologetically. 'His family had money – their name was Wallace. He inherited at least a quarter share in most of the Quinbegg boats, though Lord knows what he does with the cash that brings in. Probably keeps it under his bed in a sack. But he's important among the fishermen. And anything the damned fool starts spouting about can matter.' He sniffed disdainfully.

'Probably there's your reason why he's got such a thing on about the fishing going sour. It's costing him money.'

Carrick shook his head in a slow surprise. 'He had me fooled.'

'He has himself fooled.'

'Maybe.' Carrick wasn't so sure. 'There's some kind of fishermen's meeting scheduled for today. Heard about it?'

'No. But I can find out what happens.' Robertson gum-chewed for a moment then pointed a sudden forefinger. 'I've an idea. Come out to my place for a drink this evening, any time around seven. My wife will want to meet you and Mora Atholl will be there – company will do her good. Anything I've heard I'll tell you then. All right?'

'Fine.' Carrick got to his feet. 'We should be back in harbour by then . . . I hope.'

Robertson escorted him out into the workshop. The foreman and a mechanic had the Ford there, its front wheels jacked off the ground. They worked on for a couple of minutes then the jack sighed down.

'Ready,' said the foreman curtly.

'And no charge,' said Robertson cheerfully. 'Any trouble, Kip?'

'They seemed all right.' The man glanced balefully at Carrick. 'But we tightened them.'

Which was an understatement. Driving away, Carrick dabbed the brake-pedal for a corner ahead. The brakes gripped fiercely, the Ford shuddered – and only his grip on the steering wheel stopped him hitting the windscreen.

All of which left an uneasy feeling that Robertson's foreman didn't like unnecessary work.

He drove gingerly the rest of the way, saw the helicopter had gone from the waste ground, left the station wagon there, and went aboard the *Clavella*.

It was ten minutes before sailing time and the m.f.v.'s big diesel was already purring. Clapper Bell wasn't in sight, but Third Officer Paxton was standing near the bow lines, his bearded young face far from happy.

'Trouble?' queried Carrick, going over.

Paxton shook his head sadly. 'No – just Commander Dobie, sir. He's going around like he's ready to burst a boiler.'

Carrick didn't comment and headed straight below. He found the diminutive Chief Superintendent of Fisheries still in the wardroom, scowling over a scatter of report sheets and folders. Dobie looked up and gave a curt nod.

'Learn anything, mister?'

'A couple of things, sir.' Carrick quickly paraphrased through his conversation with Harvey Robertson and saw Dobie's eyebrows rise a fraction at the mention of Preacher Noah's fishing interests.

'Then we label him "handle with care".' Dobie pursed his lips. 'But whatever he says the men who attacked him didn't come from this crew – not unless you've a handpicked bunch of liars aboard. I've talked to them all. Their stories dovetail right through.'

'Even Peter Leslie's, sir?'

'The way I read him, he couldn't burst a paper bag in anger,' snapped Dobie irritably. He sat back with a sigh. 'Anyway, I've something more important to worry about. I went looking for John Humbey's research notes on these damned dinoflagellates. Like to guess how much I've found so far?' His hand slapped the table. 'Nothing – plenty of other junk, but nothing that matters.'

Carrick hesitated. 'Couldn't the rest of the team –'

'They know damn all.' Dobie got to his feet. 'Come and see what I'm up against.'

58

The small figure in the dark lounge suit strode from the wardroom and headed aft. Carrick followed along the narrow companionway and past the vibrating midships throb of the idling diesel, then through a bulkhead door marked 'Authorized Personnel Only'. This was research team territory, the first time he'd really penetrated the area. A large cabin which ran the full width of the ship was laid out as a fully equipped laboratory. Above the microscopes and electronic cabinets a battery of glass-fronted specimen tanks held a wriggling, darting assortment of marine life from tiny sprats to a couple of strange, hag-faced fish Carrick had never seen before. Nearby, a small, ticking electric pump was feeding a stream of air bubbles through a complicated rig of tubes and bottles.

In the middle of it all stood Peter Leslie and his two juniors. Whatever they'd been talking about before they were now silent and making a weak pretence at unconcern over this new invasion of their privacy.

Giving a glare and a grunt in Leslie's direction, Commander Dobie marched across to a row of metal cabinets and gestured along them.

'The filing system, Carrick – that's what they call it, anyway. Each man with his own key to his own section.' He scowled at Leslie. 'Tell the rest of it again.'

'A pleasure.' Leslie sounded as if he'd much rather have dumped his visitors in one of the specimen tanks, with the lid clamped down. 'All practical bench work is done here. Then we usually write report notes in our own cabins. But the final notes are always filed in these cabinets. When and how –' he shrugged – 'that's up to the individual.' He glanced at his companions for support.

'He's right, commander,' volunteered Haydock. 'It may sound unusual, but we're normally working on separate project items.'

Nodding agreement, Allison pushed the spectacles higher on his nose. 'Didn't you have any luck in Mr Humbey's cabin?'

Dobie bristled. 'Do you imagine I'd be back like this if I had?' He swung to Leslie again. 'You're sure there's only the one master key to these cabinets?'

'Just the one, and John Humbey kept it.' Leslie stroked a hand along the barrel of a heavy comparison microscope. 'You've got it now, along with the rest of his keys.'

'After they'd lain overnight in his cabin where anyone could have got at them,' grated Dobie. 'And after I'd found half the filing cabinets weren't locked anyway. What sort of security does that amount to?'

'Humbey's personal files were locked,' countered Leslie with an uneasy dignity. 'Outside of that we happen to trust each other. But Allison has an idea that might help. We use two small storerooms for'ard. Mainly they hold equipment spares but now and again Humbey would use one for special work, when he wanted extra privacy. And if this file you're looking for is so important . . .' He let his voice die away.

A sound midway between a groan and a sigh escaped from Dobie. 'Why didn't someone tell me before?' he complained testily. 'Mister Carrick –'

'Sir?'

'It's eleven hundred hours or near enough. Get this tub out of harbour and on her way. I'll try these storerooms as soon as we've cleared.'

Last man aboard, Clapper Bell came galloping down the quayside and panted over the gangway moments before it was drawn in. Still panting, the big Glasgow-Irishman waved cheerfully as he saw Carrick, then leaned against the rail in the role of an interested spectator.

Bell wasn't alone. A surprising number of people had suddenly discovered reasons to be around. With fishing boats tied three deep fore and aft, the task of easing the *Clavella* clear of her berth wouldn't be a simple one. It might even amount to an entertainment.

Prowling the wheelhouse, glad that the m.f.v.'s regular coxswain was at the helm and with a positive gratitude to Commander Dobie for being discreet enough to stay below, Carrick treated his first acquaintance of the little vessel's handling with delicate care.

He knew he had a critical audience both aboard and ashore. But full rudder, a touch of the auxiliary electric drive and a balancing play with the bow thrust unit eased her stern clear. A traumatic moment when she seemed certain to thump the bow of a seine netter passed, and a few minutes later his command was on its way out of Quinbegg harbour.

Giving a long sigh of relief he pushed the cap further back on his head, glanced aft at the Blue Ensign of the Fishery Protection squadron crackling in the wind at the stern, listened to the beat of the diesel for a moment, and relaxed.

'Hold course and speed,' he ordered. 'Take over, Sam. You know where we're going.'

Sam Paxton nodded from his post by the compass binnacle. 'Aye aye, sir. That was nicely done.'

'I was saying my prayers.' Carrick grinned at him, looked again at the receding shore, then went in search of Clapper Bell.

The bo'sun was already busy sorting out their scuba gear in the shelter of the deckhouse. He stopped work, considered Carrick with a crinkling smile then suggested hopefully, 'Feel like breakin' regulations?'

'Without witnesses.' Carrick closed the door.

Going over to his monkey-jacket, which he'd draped over one of the boxes, Bell solemnly produced a hip flask, poured a stiff measure of whisky into the cup, and handed it over.

'Thanks.' Carrick drank it at a gulp, felt the last of the tension fade from him as the whisky burned down, but shook his head at the offer of a refill. 'What else did you pick up back there?'

'In the gossip line?' Bell helped himself to a quick swallow from the flask then carefully hid it away. 'Well, the meeting o' skippers this afternoon could be nasty. Some of them want to block us out o' the harbour. Others aren't so militant. They're more in favour of tying up in protest and refusing to sail.'

'Leaving us in a jam either way,' said Carrick grimly. He knelt beside the twin cylinders now mounted on his scuba harness. Both read fully charged at 120 atmospheres, equal to 1800 pounds per square inch. 'Any more gossip?'

'Uh-huh, though I don't know if it matters.' Bell rubbed his jaw. 'I got talkin' with one bloke, which cost me a couple of beers as lubrication. He said that despite all the rumpuses Captain Jeffrey and this Preacher character seemed to stay pretty friendly. Preacher had him on his boat for quite a spell a couple o' nights back.'

'Probably trying to convert him.' Carrick mentally filed the fact though it didn't particularly connect. He balanced against a sudden roll as one sea bigger than the rest met the m.f.v. Then he got to his feet and gestured towards the equipment. 'Everything seems fine.'

'I've double-checked,' said Bell easily. 'If we forgot anything it'd be a hell of a long way to have to come back.'

Spray was breaking along the *Clavella*'s port quarter and whipping in sheets along her deck. But her broad hull took the swell without complaint, the weather forecast was reasonable, the sky was clearing, and it was the kind of fresh, gusting day Carrick could enjoy.

He reached the wheelhouse, nodded to Sam Paxton, but deliberately stayed in the background and watched him at work for a spell. The mate might be young and he'd have to learn to hone his orders a little. But he had the makings of a good deck officer. Satisfied, shutting his mind to the rest, Carrick turned his thoughts to the dive ahead.

Two hundred feet was near enough the working limit for any experienced diver using straight compressed air breathing. And the need for equalizing pressure at that depth meant the aqualung cylinders would have their air gobbled up at twice the rate for shallow water work. Plus the fact that the return to the surface would require a carefully timed series of decompression stops on the way, needed to get rid of the excess nitrogen forced into a diver's body after any deep-dive operation.

Trying to shave down these stops was for fools – and could bring an agony of pain, the classic 'bends', when the surface was reached.

No, they wouldn't have much time to spare. It would have been a lot easier if they could have been operating on one of the sophisticated oxygen and gas mixtures used by the real deep-dive specialists. But with a combination of luck and some fast work it could be done.

Carrick sucked his teeth and switched away from the possibilities as Commander Dobie appeared from the direction of the chartroom.

'How much longer, mister?' asked Dobie, who seemed mildly happier.

'Sam?' Carrick glanced towards Paxton.

'Ten, maybe fifteen minutes, sir,' replied Paxton with reasonable assurance. Fresh spray pattered against the wheelhouse glass as he added, 'We shouldn't have much trouble.'

Glad someone felt that way, Carrick turned back to Commander Dobie. 'Any luck with your own search, sir?'

'A little. Preliminary stuff – tucked away behind a pile of thermal charts that Leslie thought he'd lost.' Dobie growled deep in his throat. 'These research wonders live in a shambles all their own. Still, at least they've come up with one thing that'll help you.' He rubbed his hands together, peering ahead. 'It's an underwater TV camera. We can use it before you go down.'

Carrick whistled appreciatively. 'I didn't know they had one!'

'You'll find most things on a research ship,' countered Dobie acidly. 'At least, if you try hard enough. Normally the thing is only for shallow water scanning. But they're rigging longer cables. It should work.'

The hand-buoy markers, three small, anchored floats with fluttering signal pennants, were spotted by an oilskin-clad lookout just before Sam Paxton's fifteen minute estimate expired. For the m.f.v.'s crew, accustomed to pin-point underwater observation, the next stage was smooth routine.

Diesel cut back to a mutter, echo-sounder registering on fine scale, they used the markers as a centre-point for a gradually widening sweep. The graph recorder's needle tracked a flat, regular seabed, fuzzing only occasionally in a way expertly dismissed as a passing shoal of fish. Then, suddenly, it jerked in a firm, positive peak.

Coming round, they registered the same peak again.

'Just under thirty-five fathoms – two hundred and

ten feet.' Dobie nodded. 'Let's see what your camera thing can do, Leslie.'

It was Haydock and Allison's 'camera thing'. Monitor screen and camera controls were located in a small booth aft of the exhaust stack. With the *Clavella* creeping round again under little more than steerage way the camera's blimp-like housing was lowered beneath the white-capped waves. As the tube warmed a picture formed – dull despite the power of the camera's halogen lamp, swaying slightly with the roll of the vessel above.

For a moment the screen showed a bare, empty undersea desert of grey sediment flecked by a few bushy patches of wrack weed. Then Haydock gave a whoop and pointed. A shadowy outline was appearing in the background.

Peering over his shoulder Carrick watched the outline firm as they edged nearer.

'She's a mess,' said Haydock in a new, subdued voice.

Carrick nodded. They had the submersible. But if she was shaped like an overweight glider she'd also crashed like one. Port stub-wing broken off, she lay with her nose half-buried in the seabed – and as he watched, the picture from below began to break up and the screen went blank.

'Sorry,' apologized Allison. 'The camera wasn't built for this kind of depth. The pressure down there is –' He stopped and grinned weakly. 'Well, you don't need us to tell you about it.'

'No,' agreed Carrick wryly.

But the camera had more than earned its keep. The contact was confirmed and he knew what he was up against. Already changed into his black rubber scuba suit, he left the control booth and quickly went aft. Similarly ready, Clapper Bell was there taking a last few drags at a cigarette. At the stern, the winch drum began rumbling and the heavy trawl warp, hooked salvage chains on its shackle end, started to slide down.

Flicking the cigarette away, Bell helped Carrick into one of the heavy aqualung harnesses then effortlessly shrugged his way into his own. As they made last adjustments to the straps Commander Dobie came over.

'Ready?' asked Dobie.

Carrick nodded, spat on the glass of his face-mask, rubbed it over, then rinsed the result in a waiting bucket of water. De-mist sprays didn't come better. Pulling on the face-mask and biting the mouthpiece he followed Clapper Bell to the low deck-rail.

They waited for the *Clavella*'s next roll then went over backward together.

Chapter Four

'Wet' scuba suits are just that. They trap a layer of water under their rubber and use it as a fluid insulation between the wearer's body and the outside temperature. And the sea comes cold off Scotland's north-west coast.

The familiar initial chill hit Carrick as the green water closed above his head. He let himself sink deeper, the dark hull of the m.f.v. above, Clapper Bell a little below and to his right. Then he signalled and they began finning down, twin trails of air bubbles pluming from their masks.

Regulator valve clicking steadily, legs moving in a smooth crawl-beat, Carrick used the descending trawl warp as a guide while the water around gradually lost its brightness and began to filter to a dull blue. He passed a convoy of slow-moving semi-transparent jellyfish, pulsing their way with a few young cod and haddock travelling in the shelter of their long, trailing tentacles. As they vanished a warning pain began building up behind his eyes. He forced air from his mouth up into the face-piece area. The pain faded as the pressure was equalized and the rest was a discipline of regular breathing and unhurried pace. The grim humour of the naval diving course put the alternative well. Rush or hold your breath on the way down if you want. But leave the name of your next of kin and save the paperwork later.

The blue became darker, the seabed shaped below. When the depth gauge strapped to one wrist quivered towards the two hundred foot mark he twisted round and almost drifted the last distance. The rubber flippers on his feet barely stirred the bottom sediment as they touched. Already there, Clapper Bell came closer and signalled energetically.

Ploughed deep, exposing pebbled clay but already beginning to fill again, a giant skid-mark ran at an angle across the bottom where the submersible had come to rest. A dozen strokes took them over. As Bell's weight-belt bumped the metal a small, startled fish darted from the shattered interior and fled in terror.

It was among the lucky ones. This was dinoflagellate territory. Here and there the floor of the sea showed a fleck of dull silver or fading red which didn't move and wouldn't again, casualties of the invading bloom, left to be scavenged by the crawling bottom creatures . . . those that were left.

Carrick concentrated on the submersible, the bubble-plumes of each exhaled breath as effective as any time-clock. He moved round slowly, checking its length, frowning a little.

The prospect wasn't encouraging. Cockpit area ruptured open and splayed back in a way that held its own significance, the main weight of the nose-down unit seemed to be resting on the broken root of the port stub-wing. But whether she could be recovered with moderate ease depended on something else, the maintenance lifting points. According to his briefing there should be one under the base of each wing.

Hand-holding over the canted metal, Carrick found the starboard lug. Its eyelet was sturdy and undamaged, and he moved round to the other side. Clapper Bell was already there, crouching low on the bottom clay and scowling through his face-mask as he pointed. The port root was buried deep in the seabed, its lug somewhere below.

Twisting his body as he came, Carrick landed beside Bell, grimaced, tapped the broad-bladed diving knife in his companion's leg-sheath then sign-talked the rest. A larger than usual spurt of air bubbles vented the bo'sun's feeling but he eased over and drew his knife.

Side by side, using the steel blades as spades, they set to work. But it was far from easy. The clay was firmly packed, every other stab into it seemed to jar against hidden pebbles, and forcing any kind of lever-age became a growing effort. Still they burrowed on, fingers numbed and swollen, working in a low, swirling mist of bottom sediment, until the port lug was finally exposed.

It was intact. Relieved, they sank back and rested a moment before the next and crucial stage. The trawl warp from the *Clavella* was a quivering, waiting snake of black not many yards away, its end chains occa-sionally stirring on the bottom as if they had a life of their own.

The chains were heavy. It took a combined effort to drag them over and lock their hooks into the lifting eyelets. Fingers gashed and bleeding, moving with an unaccustomed clumsiness, Carrick was exhausted as they finished and finned clear. It took a positive effort to extract the first of the special smoke-flare cartridges from his weight-belt pouch, tug the release ring, then toss the squat cylinder away from him.

Gas-generated, the cartridge shot upward. A minute later, which meant only seconds after the orange surface-smoke must have been spotted, the trawl warp quivered with a new life. First the chains jerked and tightened then a great grey cloud of sediment swirled like a blinding fog as the submersible was heaved clear of the seabed. As it rose, dragged by the

Clavella's winch drum, it swung wildly and briefly then began travelling steadily.

Watching it vanish, Carrick felt a tap on his shoulder. Clapper Bell, his face-plate only inches away, winked and thumbed upward. He nodded a thankful agreement and began finning up again through the gradually lightening water.

It began as an odd tugging sensation against his body as he swam. Then a quivering vibration which became a puzzling pull. Before realization could dawn, Carrick suddenly felt himself tossed and thrown by a giant, invisible force.

Tumbled head over heels, swept along powerless to resist, he had a fractional glimpse of a grotesque thrashing of arms and legs as Clapper Bell's black-suited figure whirled by. Then he was being rushed on, part of an increasing horizontal maelstrom of tossing debris and struggling, living flotsam. Dark strands of torn kelp-weed slapped as he fought to regain some kind of balance. A rubber flipper was torn from his foot and a twisting, helplessly angry conger eel gyrated inches away from his face-plate glass before it vanished. All round he glimpsed the frantic shapes of trapped fish, large and small. A massive balk of driftwood banged his arm and spun sideways.

They were in the grip of the same invisible captor. Carrick knew what it meant, felt a chill of fear at what he had to fight, and cursed his own carelessness at not having guessed the possibility.

It had been there on the charts, on the sprinkled, regularly marked soundings. Combine tidal overfall with undersea currents and the result can be one of nature's deadliest traps. He was in one now – a sudden, sweeping thermal of water pouring into this seabed valley from the shallower areas around, a sandwich filling of tempestuous energy wakened to furious life.

70

Above and below the sea might be unchanged. But within its layer and particularly at the edges was a world of rushing turmoil. Depth and width could be anything, length a short distance or long miles. The wrist compass showed he was being carried in a north-west direction, straight for the open Atlantic. And when the current dissipated, as its grip relaxed –

Far out at sea he'd seen whole tree trunks shoot suddenly and unexpectedly to the surface from nightmare depths. Tree trunks which had fallen back to float scarred and battered from some fantastic underwater journey. To avoid that, to get out before his air supply was exhausted, he would have to fight. Fight down panic first, let himself go with the current yet again towards the surface.

Small, squirming, unseen shapes bumped against Carrick as he strained his whole being to swim upward. Body trimmed like a kite, every stroke was a separate battle. Then, at last, forty feet won by the depth gauge, he almost welcomed the new and broken feel of the water around. The top edge of the layer, the final barrier, was the enemy which now sucked and clawed alternately at everything from the breathing mask to the legs of his suit.

In his weakened state a new temptation offered. He could release the lead-filled weight-belt round his waist and gain positive buoyancy from the air tanks. But once he broke clear the same positive buoyancy would send him upwards at such a rate that he'd go straight through the next and vital decompression stop.

Rejecting the notion, forcing concentration, knowing he had scant energy remaining, Carrick mustered his screaming muscles for a final attack and kicked upward. Hammering, tearing forces pounded his body and all sense of reality faded, leaving only a mechanical determination.

71

Then, as suddenly as it had begun, it ended and he was through to calm green water. The depth gauge read fifty feet and a small squid was peacefully propelling along just above.

Floating almost motionless he took his first decompression stop – a long one, longer than any diving table ordained but one his body desperately needed after its ordeal.

On the last stage he was working on the emergency air reserve. Breaking surface in the hollow of a wave he rode high on the crest of the next, saw a boat's hull for an instant before he dropped down in the following hollow, and quickly triggered another of the smoke cartridges.

Rising in a belching column, the orange smoke was answered quickly by the bray of a klaxon horn. With a sound very close to a sob Carrick cracked the CO_2 capsule which inflated his lifejacket.

When he opened his eyes again the fishing boat was close alongside. Strong arms hauled him aboard, he was propped up on the slippery deck amid loud, excited comments, then a bottle was unceremoniously rammed between his lips. He swallowed instinctively, coughed, spluttered on the neat whisky, and began to shiver uncontrollably.

'Don't gi' him any more,' protested an aggrieved Highland voice. 'He'll do now. An' that's the only bottle I've got.' Then, above the steady beat of the boat's paraffin engine, the same voice groaned. 'God almighty – there's another o' them popped up. An' I'll wager he'll be wanting a dram too. Hey, skipper –'

Still shivering but beginning to feel distinctly better, Carrick was able to muster a grin as Clapper Bell was shortly yanked aboard in turn and dumped beside him. The bo'sun's feeble cursing ended as the bottle was offered and he gulped from it in uninhibited style. A new lament arose from the owner – one that sounded as sweet as any music to Carrick's ears.

But the distant coastline was strange and there was no sign of the *Clavella*. He asked their position, heard it almost without believing then glanced at his diving watch. Allowing time for all the rest he and Clapper had probably been in that current for no more than fifteen minutes. Yet in that fifteen minutes they'd been swept almost five miles.

They were aboard the seine netter *Kirtle Lass*, a Mallaig boat on her way home with a full fish-hold after working around the Butt of Lewis. Her skipper, a grizzled, unshaven and tired-eyed man, radioed the *Clavella* and arranged a rendezvous as soon as he'd made sure the latest additions to his catch were relatively intact.

'Aye, a wee shade unusual,' was his comment about it all when he heard how they'd arrived. Wrapped in borrowed blankets, Carrick and Bell had been crammed beside him in the relative warmth of the tiny wheelhouse. 'Still, that's the sort o' thing you're paid for, I suppose.'

A loud grunt from Clapper Bell made him chuckle, then he remembered his duties as host. 'Have another taste o' Sandy's bottle if you want. He won't mind.'

'I'm not so sure,' said Carrick, grinning in turn and shaking his head. 'Skipper, we owe you a lot. If you hadn't been around –'

'Och, you wouldn't have had too long to wait,' assured the fisherman. 'There's a foreign boat – one o' the big Russkie trawlers – not far at the back of us.' He turned and looked astern then frowned a little. 'Or he was, anyway.'

'You're sure?' Glancing back, Carrick saw only empty sea. He accepted the skipper's nod with

73

minimal curiosity. Russian boats were no novelty. Like the Poles and East Germans they regularly joined other European fleets working the open water and frequently came close inshore for a variety of purposes. As long as they didn't try to fish within the limits and obeyed the usual rules they were an accepted if not particularly welcome part of the scenery. 'Any idea where he'd be heading?'

'None.' The fisherman rocked on his heels to the boat's slow, fish-heavy roll. 'Still, there's not many craft come this way. Nearer Quinbegg or to the south, where the fishing's good, it can be like a flamin' city traffic jam at times. But not this stretch.' He stopped, his gaze suddenly quizzical. 'Though there's word that the fishing around Quinbegg has gone a wee bittie sour. Would that be true?'

'They've had a few problems,' parried Carrick. The *Clavella* was in sight, the gap between them narrowing rapidly. And at least one part had gone all right. The salvaged submersible was plainly visible, secured to the m.f.v.'s tall stern gantry posts.

'Aye.' It came with a tranquil satisfaction. 'Then if they're low on catches at Quinbegg the Mallaig market prices should be rising. And we hit a grand patch o' fat herring this trip.'

There was always an angle, decided Carrick.

Commander Dobie had an angle of his own. He waited with an effort till Carrick and Clapper Bell had been transferred aboard from the *Kirtle Lass* and the fishing boat had edged away again to resume her journey south. Then, hands on hips, an outraged little figure, he exploded his anger.

'You could have been damned well killed down there. What kind of a mess would that have left, eh?'

Carrick swallowed. But Clapper Bell was supremely unruffled. He queried innocently, 'You mean you'd have missed us, sir?'

For a moment Dobie's mouth twitched uncertainly. Then his voice rasped again. 'Do you know what you tangled with down there? A twenty-knot thermal layer, one of the worst damned undersea tidal races on the whole coast. What's more, do you know who could have forecast to the exact minute when it would begin – if he hadn't forgotten all about it in the general hubbub?' A visibly quivering finger pointed to a group gathered aft. 'That damned fool Leslie. Practically his sole reason for being aboard has been to study the patterns around here.'

'Just when did he remember?' asked Carrick in grim, weary voice.

'As soon as we started getting vibrations when we were lifting the submersible.' Dobie winced at the reminder. 'Did I say vibrations? It was swinging like a berserk pendulum, practically tore the whole blasted stern away. And all the time that was happening I was stuck with a mate who could only stand with his mouth hanging open and that idiot Leslie running around wringing his hands and saying how sorry he was!'

'Maybe I'll make him feel sorrier,' grated Carrick in a voice he hardly recognized as his own. But it wouldn't be straight away. His limbs were like lead, the rubber clinging to his body felt as though it would have to be peeled, he was groggy and hardly cared who knew it.

Dobie saw the signs, frowned, and changed his mood as if throwing a switch.

'Get below,' he said shortly. 'Both of you – and stay there. You've earned your keep for a spell.'

It was as near as they were likely to get to a compliment.

Once in his cabin Carrick stripped off the scuba suit, forced his bruised body to stay under the hot needles of the shower for a couple of minutes, then dried

75

himself roughly and slumped down on the bunk. Within moments he was asleep and oblivious to the quickening throb as the motor fishing vessel swung round on her new course, heading south.

What finally wakened him was the sheer lack of motion. Carrick lay back, eyelids still gummed, uncertain what was wrong, puzzled by the strange noises which seemed to be coming from outside. Then, realization dawning, he levered up on his elbows and stared out of the cabin porthole.

The *Clavella* was back in Quinbegg, tied alongside the quay. A massive articulated transporter with Royal Navy badges on the truck cab was reversing a few feet away and the rest of the noise was compounded from the harsh clatter of the deck winch and a variety of shouted instructions. Sam Paxton was ashore, dancing with anxiety as he guided the transporter nearer to the edge of the quay.

Fumbling for his cigarettes and automatically lighting one, Carrick swung down from the bunk and winced at what that did to his aching muscles. The hands of his watch were leaving six p.m. which meant he'd been asleep for more than a couple of hours. A couple of hours when anything could have been happening – he dressed quickly, cursed his gashed fingertips as he made a clumsy job of shirt buttons and tie, then hurried out.

As he reached the deck he collided with the wiry, overalled shape of Willie Dewar. The engineer grinned at his muttered apology.

'You're supposed to be snug in your pit, chief,' declared Dewar cheerfully. 'Man, you still look pretty hellish.'

'That's how I feel,' said Carrick absently, frowning aft. They'd already begun swinging the salvaged submersible out and over towards the transporter truck. 'How long since we got back?'

76

'Twenty minutes. Your pal Bell is still snorin' his head off below. If you want him –'

'Let him enjoy it.' Carrick shook his head. Up on the quayside Commander Dobie was beckoning in his direction. Leaving Dewar, he strode over the gangway to where Dobie stood waiting.

'I was going to send for you,' said Dobie without preliminaries. 'Once that thing is loaded I'm on my way.' He scowled at the renewed clatter of the winch and gestured towards the waste ground beyond the quay. The Department helicopter had returned. 'Department want a personal report – they're being pressured from higher up.'

Carrick raised a surprised eyebrow. 'Have you got all you need for them, sir?'

'No.' It came harshly. Dobie glared at the few fishermen and villagers who were hanging around and had to raise his voice above the general din. 'But I'll be back to try again in the morning – alone if possible, though I'd say that's doubtful.'

The submersible swung amid a crescendo of effort from the winch and a squeal of pulleys. Then it lowered, the weight of metal meeting the transporter's platform in a way which made the road springs sag. Immediately a team of the *Clavella*'s seamen draped a tarpaulin over the shattered nose section and started to lash it down for the journey ahead.

'I hoped I'd have a chance to look it over first,' murmured Carrick, watching.

'The sooner we get the thing south the sooner the technical people can get to work,' grunted Dobie. 'If it's any consolation I've already gone through it with Dewar. Behind that sandpaper face he's a pretty good engineer. We found enough to work out our own theory.'

'Sir?' Carrick sensed the anger behind the words.

'There was a bomb aboard all right. There's all the signs of an explosion in the keel ballast compartment, where there should have been nothing but a layer of lead weights.' Dobie reached into his pocket and produced a twisted stub of copper tubing now wrapped in a plastic bag. 'This was among the debris. It doesn't look much, but I'd say it is what's left of a pressure-operated detonator – the homemade equivalent of a depth-charge detonator. That ballast compartment isn't watertight. In fact, it has hinged doors so that the lead weights can be dumped. You follow me, mister?'

Slowly, Carrick nodded. If the bomb had been placed in the ballast compartment, primed by the pressure detonator, then nothing would have happened until the submersible went into a dive and reached deep enough water for the pressure below to activate it.

'An amateur wouldn't be able to build that kind of device,' he said quietly. 'Even getting it into the ballast compartment would be tricky.'

'I know. But it happened.' Suddenly the older man's voice sounded very tired. Putting the bag away again, Dobie shrugged. 'There's more – none of it good. At least half of John Humbey's research notes on the dinoflagellates seem to be missing. And I can't find as much as a hint of what Andy Jeffrey was getting so worked up about.'

'His kit –'

'Is in the wardrobe in your cabin,' completed Dobie. He managed a faint smile. 'I checked. You were lying there like a log while I went through his suitcases. No, I've a horrible feeling that someone has beaten me to it.'

'Then the seafire data and anything else could be ashore?'

'Ashore – maybe on their way somewhere.' Dobie looked at him gravely. 'That's what I've got to tell

Department when I get back, and there's going to be hell to pay in several directions.' His hands spread in a gesture of wry resignation. 'Well, any ideas, mister?'

Carrick frowned. 'The skipper on the *Kirtle Lass* talked about a trawler –'

'The Russian?' Dobie wasn't impressed. 'Probably coincidence. Plenty of them stray this way for perfectly ordinary reasons. But – all right, I'll have her checked. You're seeing Robertson again?'

'This evening.'

'Then pump him harder. Maybe you could try Preacher Noah too. Scratch around – that's about all we can do.' Dobie stopped and fell silent as Sam Paxton hurried over.

'Transporter ready to leave, sir,' reported the young mate breathlessly. 'Will I let him go?'

Dobie nodded, Paxton trotted back, signalled to the transporter driver, and the big articulated rig grated into gear. As it slowly rumbled past them, heading for the main road, Dobie beckoned Carrick again and began walking toward the helicopter.

Along the quayside the moored boats rocked gently in the faint swell, their decks deserted. Nearer the shore, where the tidal mud began, there was a new scattering of dead and dying fish. Half-covered by silt, the body of a herring gull lay with one wing spread grotesquely over a rusted oil drum.

'At least we haven't had a fishermen's deputation along cursing us,' mused Carrick. 'Not yet, anyway – when I see Preacher I can have a go at stalling off trouble from that direction.'

'Try it,' said Dobie tersely. 'We've enough on our plate.' He pursed his lips and stopped, shivering a little in the light wind. 'Mister, understand this plainly. We could be up against someone ashore or someone aboard – or both. I'm changing my mind about one thing. Keep an eye on Peter Leslie. He was your hunch earlier. Now he's mine.'

Carrick shrugged. 'Right now I'm biased in that direction. Clapper Bell feels the same.'

'He could have forgotten about the current in the general excitement.' Dobie made a reluctant attempt at impartiality. 'All that would rate is a good kick on the backside. But if he didn't forget –' he shook his head – 'no, there's nothing positive we can put against him. But I'm finished taking chances in that direction. He's top of my list when I get back.'

The helicopter's engine came to life and the rotors began to turn. Grimacing, Dobie gave a final nod and hurried over. His small figure was scarcely aboard the machine before the blades quickened and the engine's note built up to a roar. Seconds later it lifted, began climbing, and swung out to cross over the bay.

Hands deep in his pockets, still pondering over Dobie's warning, Webb Carrick decided against returning immediately to the *Clavella* and made his way round toward the outer basin.

His luck seemed in. Long black jacket flapping loose, Preacher Noah was working on the deck of his boat. He looked up as Carrick hailed him, slowly laid down the lobster creel he'd been baiting, and waited with a show of impatience while his visitor scrambled down the iron ladder set in the stonework.

'Got a moment to spare?' asked Carrick as he stepped aboard.

'No more than that.' Fastening the jacket buttons, Preacher gestured towards a stacked heap of creels lying in the well of the boat. 'I've these to lay before the tide turns, and a fair distance to sail if there's to be half a chance of catching anything.'

The creels were old but well maintained. Carrick nodded appreciatively. 'I didn't know you worked a lobster line.'

'I'm obliging a friend.' The gaunt face stayed impassive. 'What do you want, Carrick?'

'Some idea of what happened at the skippers' meeting. Did they decide anything?'

'Only that they disagreed about what to do.' Preacher's thin shoulders twitched in a shrug. 'There will be another meeting tomorrow. When a decision is reached your people will hear soon enough.'

Sighing, Carrick shoved his cap another inch back on his forehead and considered the man hopefully. 'Suppose I tell you there's a reasonable, natural explanation for what's happening on the fishing grounds. Suppose I give you my word the *Clavella* isn't in any way responsible, that her research team are – well, trying to find a cure? Doesn't that make a difference?'

'I heard the same thing from Captain Jeffrey.' Preacher folded his arms stubbornly. 'I asked him for proof but it didn't come. Can you do better?'

'Not yet, but soon.'

'Then I'll wait till it happens.' Preacher's deep-set blue eyes narrowed perceptibly. 'I hear something else which interests me more – that you came close to drowning this afternoon.' His lips pursed briefly and solemnly. 'Close enough for it to be another warning. You were luckier than your friend Captain Jeffrey – but you might not be next time.'

'I'll take that chance,' said Carrick bluntly. 'Preacher, I've heard a few things too. Including the fact that if you told the skippers they should hold off for a couple of days they'd obey without a murmur. Why don't you give me that much – against the promise of the proof you want at the end of it?'

'I might think about it.' Turning deliberately, Preacher nodded at the level of water on the basin's

81

wall. 'My opinion is man thinks best when he is alone – and sailing.'

'All right.' Carrick took the hint, swung back on to the iron ladder, and climbed to the top. When he looked down, Preacher Noah was calmly busy with the lobster creels.

Somehow Carrick had a feeling he hadn't failed. Commander Dobie would have been apoplectic if he'd been there to hear that promise of proof. Whether he could do it was something which dug hard against Carrick's conscience. But if he won those two days it would at least mean a breathing space.

When he reached the *Clavella* he asked the seaman on gangway duty if Clapper Bell was still aboard. The man thought so but wasn't sure and Carrick left it at that, heading for his cabin. The door was closed. He opened it, then stopped with his mouth half-open in surprise.

Bell was there, towering angrily over a badly frightened Peter Leslie. The research officer sat on the edge of the bunk, using a handkerchief to dab shakily at a badly split lip.

'What the blazes is going on?' demanded Carrick, coming in and quickly closing the door again.

'Carrick, I –' Rising to his feet, Leslie broke off with a yelp as Clapper Bell placed a massive hand against his blue kapok jacket and shoved him down again.

'I came in an' caught him pawing through your stuff,' said Bell shortly. 'He nearly had a canary when he saw me, then there was a wee bit o' awkwardness before he decided to stay.'

The wardrobe door lay open. One of Andy Jeffrey's suitcases had been dragged out and its contents were still spilled on the floor. Carrick's face hardened.

'Leslie?'

'I –' Leslie dabbed again at his lip – 'I'd lost something. It might have been in here, that's all. It was –

well, just a mistake. But this damned gorilla of yours wouldn't listen.'

Bell chuckled derisively. 'The only mistake was he let himsel' get caught.'

'Clapper –' Carrick frowned him silent. 'This "something" you lost, Leslie. Tell me about it.'

'It was a book, one Captain Jeffrey might have borrowed. But it – it isn't important.' Leslie swallowed hard. 'Look, I'm sorry. I apologize. But there's no need for an inquisition. Carrick, if you forget about it I'll forget about Bell hitting me. Let's leave it at that.'

'Like hell we will,' snapped Carrick. Crossing over, he gripped Leslie by the front of his grey sweater and jerked him to his feet. 'So you came looking for a book? That's so lame it amounts to an insult. I'll tell you what happened. You saw me going ashore with Commander Dobie and decided it was a perfect chance to sneak along. What's wrong? Haven't you collected enough of the seafire data yet?' He released his grip and gave a gesture of contempt. 'Or were you looking for something different – something Andy Jeffrey might have hidden that could finish you if it was found?'

'That's a mad idea!' Leslie's face twitched nervously. 'Carrick, I've been helping –'

'Like you did at the Quinbegg Trench this afternoon?'

The man gave a sound like a moan and shook his head. 'I forgot about that current, I swear it. There's been so much else, too much.' He closed his eyes, his whole body shaking with emotion. 'Damn this ship. *Clavella* – yes, it's well named. Do you know what *Clavella* means to a marine biologist? I'll tell you. It's a small, nasty variety of fish parasite. Someone with a sense of humour thought it fitted here – and God, how right they were!'

83

Bewildered, Clapper Bell blinked at them. 'What's he goin' on about?'

'I could make a guess,' answered Carrick softly. 'Leslie –' he waited till the man opened his eyes – 'how long have you known exactly what John Humbey's research programme was about?' He saw the answer in the way the thin lips tightened. 'Look, because I wear a uniform it doesn't mean I'm some kind of robot. I can understand if the biological warfare angle hit you in the conscience. But maybe you only know half the story.'

'Half?' It came with a quivering, bitter amusement. 'How much of it do you know? Everything has an angle for some people. Even a job like mine.' Leslie's voice cracked. 'At least John Humbey was allowed to know what he was doing.'

'Meaning?'

Sucking his gashed lip, Leslie shook his head. 'I've said enough. I – unless you object I'm going back to my cabin.'

'Those research notes first,' said Carrick. 'And anything else you've collected.'

Leslie glared at him with a new defiance. 'I say I haven't got them and I already helped Dobie go through my files. So where do we go from there?'

Wishing he knew, Carrick didn't answer. If he gauged Peter Leslie anything near correctly the research officer had a stubborn streak deep down and they'd reached it. Some people were like that. They might crack on the surface but you could beat their heads off before they'd surrender their fundamental determination, particularly when they believed in what they were doing. As he was pretty sure Leslie did.

'Sir.' Clapper Bell was over at the porthole, an odd expression on his rugged face. 'Better take a look. We've got a visitor.'

84

Frowning, Carrick went over. Mora Atholl's white MG hardtop had stopped on the quay. The girl had left it and was walking towards the *Clavella's* gangway.

'Know her?' queried Bell.

'Yes. She was Andy Jeffrey's girl.' Carrick pursed his lips, almost glad of the interruption. 'All right, Clapper. Take Leslie to his cabin, search it thoroughly for papers of any kind, then lock him in and put a guard on the door. He'll keep till Dobie gets back.'

'Aye aye, sir,' said Bell with an unaccustomed formality. Then he demanded, 'What about you?'

'I've some people to see. Though it could be a waste of time now.' He eyed Leslie coldly. 'I'd reckon you've enough equipment aboard to turn out most gadgets. How much do you know about pressure fuses?'

'Me?' Leslie blinked then suddenly understood. 'Oh no, Carrick – don't try that one. That's the biggest mistake you could make.' He sucked his lip again, latent misery in his voice. 'John Humbey was still a friend. I didn't sabotage that submersible – I haven't killed anyone.'

Carrick sighed, nodded to Clapper Bell, and left them.

Mora Atholl hadn't got past the seaman on gangway watch when Carrick reached them.

'Good,' she said with a smile of relief. 'I was beginning to wonder what to do next. Your crew don't budge easily.'

'He had orders, no visitors.' Carrick nodded at the seaman, who grinned awkwardly and eased away. 'I didn't expect you, Mora. I'm sorry.'

'No need.' She wore a plain dark blue wool two-piece, equally plain walking shoes and a minimum of make-up. He didn't ask why but she seemed to read

85

his thoughts and flushed a little. 'I don't believe in mourning, but –' She shrugged. 'Anyway, why I'm here is I told Harvey Robertson I'd drive over and collect you.'

'Already?' Carrick glanced at his watch, saw it was nearly seven, and managed a chuckle. 'I hadn't forgotten. But if you take me out how do I get back?'

'Same way, unless women drivers worry you.' Without waiting for an answer she led the way to the car.

Inside the MG was a low, compact world of black leather, an impressive instrument layout and purposeful, sports-styled controls. Envying the way Mora slid behind the wheel, Carrick crammed himself into the passenger seat, glanced appreciatively at the way the wool skirt now showed a long, nyloned expanse of firm thigh, then settled back.

She took the sports car away smoothly, one hand resting lightly on the stubby gear-shift, using a warning blip of the throttle to shift a couple of small boys from their path. The car swung out of the harbour area and began accelerating at a brisk pace through the village.

He watched her for a moment. Handling the wheel with an easy confidence, Mora seemed quietly relaxed and to have her emotions under strict control. Not all the sparkle she'd shown at their first meeting had returned but the initial reaction to Andy Jeffrey's death was obviously well behind her. He caught himself being glad, for purely selfish reasons, that this dark-haired girl hadn't been too closely involved with Jeffrey.

'Robertson said you were moving in with them,' he said at last. 'Everything all right there?'

'Fine.' She kept her eyes on the road. 'His wife is a gem, and they've the kind of house I've only seen in magazine supplements.' Changing gear, she took the

86

MG round a steep, curving rise which marked the end of the village. 'Webb, have you –'

'Found out more?' Carrick finished it for her. 'Yes, enough to be positive. Somebody put a bomb aboard it. But we've got to keep that quiet for now.'

'At least you warned me.' Her fingers went knuckle-white on the wheel. 'Can I help?'

'I'm not sure.' Carrick eased round a little in his seat. 'The last time Andy telephoned did he say anything that seemed – well, unusual?'

'That's what I've been trying to remember, ever since last night.' She shook her head slowly, almost angrily. 'He did say something, some odd kind of joke. I just can't recall what it was about – and I've tried hard enough. Yet I've a feeling it might matter if only –' She sighed.

'It'll come,' said Carrick.

At least he hoped it would. However things might look he had a growing hunch that Peter Leslie was only a beginning of what was wrong at Quinbegg.

Settling back, very conscious of the perfumed warmth of her nearness, he watched the road slip by.

Chapter Five

Harvey Robertson's home was five miles north of Quinbegg, where a narrow, pebbled track led off the main road towards the shore. The MG turned down it, bounced in bottom gear over the rough surface, then skirted a final rise of ground and emerged within a stone's throw of the house.

Fascinated, Webb Carrick leaned forward. Built hard against the living rock of a low cliff, only a shelving stretch of glistening shingle beach separating it from the water's edge, the garage owner's home was a white split-level bungalow with a flat roof and broad picture windows which faced towards a panoramic view of the North Minch. At any time that view would have been eye-catching, but the setting sun made it appear a lapping sea of golden fire.

'Like?' asked Mora with a dry amusement.

'I'd settle for it any day.' While the car purred on to halt at a gravelled parking area he noted how a concrete slipway led from a basement boathouse across the shingle. And though it sat so near the water the bungalow was well sheltered from the elements. On the landward side the rising cliff should protect it from the worst of gales. A few hundred yards out, a long hog-back ridge of black obsidian rock formed a natural barrier to the open sea.

'Six rooms, double garage and that boathouse.' Mora sighed enviously. She switched off the engine and climbed out. 'Come on. Drooling doesn't do any good.'

The main door of the house swung open as they crunched across the gravel. Waving a greeting, casually dressed in tan slacks and a dark red sports shirt, Harvey Robertson nudged his companion forward.

'Glad you could make it, Carrick,' he declared brusquely. 'Eleanor, meet the man I've been talking about.'

Eleanor Robertson was small, plump, and in her late forties, and she smiled shyly as she shook hands. Her mousey hair was well groomed but the heather-toned tweed suit she wore didn't help what remained of her figure.

'I was sorry to hear what happened,' she said in a soft sympathetic voice. 'That's why I'm particularly glad Mora could come here. But –' she glanced at the girl – 'I'm always glad of company whatever the reason.'

They were led through to a broad, open-plan lounge. It had that picture-window view, teak plank flooring and a scatter of deep, chintz-covered arm-chairs. Robertson took station beside a table with bottles and glasses, his plump, sallow face showing a growing impatience as his wife fussed over seating her guests.

'That's enough, Eleanor,' he said shortly. 'By the time you finished a man could have died of thirst. Carrick, what will it be?'

With the drinks dispensed, Robertson's manner mellowed again. Leaning over the back of a chair, glass in hand, he asked, 'Well, what do you think of our place?'

'It's a surprise, a real surprise.' Carrick nodded towards the window. 'Plenty of people would pay a fortune for that view alone.' He glanced at Eleanor Robertson. 'It must make quite a change after city life.'

'I wouldn't go back,' she said fervently. 'Not unless –'

'Unless I asked her,' finished Robertson. He gave a deep chuckle. 'Well, that's not likely to happen – not when the little green men are waiting for me down south. Anyway, I bought this place for less than half you'd pay for the average city flat.' He sipped his drink. 'How did your salvage job make out, Carrick?'

'There were problems,' said Carrick cautiously. 'But we managed.'

'Good.' Robertson dismissed the matter. 'Still interested in that skippers' meeting?'

Carrick nodded. 'I saw Preacher at the harbour. He said they can't make up their minds.'

'That's right. Didn't expect them to – nothing ever happens in a hurry around Quinbegg.' Robertson's sallow face twisted derisively. 'Up here, *mañana* would rate as an emergency. But the way I heard it the same Preacher sat on the fence this once – and as long as he stays there the rest won't decide on anything definite.'

'It certainly suits us,' murmured Carrick. 'What's your forecast?'

'Preacher's unpredictable,' grunted Robertson. 'You're on safer ground with the weather – and if you're interested, the locals are certain there's a storm on the way. They're usually right.'

Mora leaned forward. 'Mrs Robertson, what's it like here when the weather's rough?'

'Exciting. In fact, I'm glad I'm back for it.' The woman beamed. 'Between the noise of it all and the waves exploding over the long rock out there – you'll see what I mean.' Her face saddened. 'Captain Jeffrey asked the same thing the last time he was out. Remember, Harvey? It was when we had that argument about Vietnam.'

'When you had,' corrected Robertson, frowning. 'Carrick, she may not look it but my wife's the oldest hippy in the business. Make love, not war – that's her motto. When we were in London she used to be a volunteer committee worker for some high-powered nuclear disarmament mob, all beads and brotherhood. Keeps up with them still – wears her protest marches like battle honours.'

She coloured. 'That's an exaggeration –'

'Then we'll leave it,' said Robertson curtly. He finished his drink, laid down the glass, and gestured at the window. 'Getting dark out there. If you'd like a look around we'd better do it now. And you'll stay for a meal?'

'Sorry.' Carrick smiled regretfully. 'I'll need to get back – there is too much work waiting.'

'Then some other time,' shrugged Robertson. 'Anything special happening?'

'No, it's mostly routine.' Carrick cupped his glass in both hands. 'But you could maybe save me time. There's a foreign trawler wandering somewhere near – do they often come this way?'

Robertson blinked. 'Never into Quinbegg, if that's what you mean. But they sometimes shelter in bays to the north if they need repairs. If the storm forecast is right, that could be your explanation for this one.' He glanced at his wife. 'Coming on the tour?'

She shook her head. 'I'll stay in the kitchen – I'll need to, if we're going to eat. But take Mora with you.'

They left the woman still sipping her drink. Shepherded along, Carrick obediently looked into rooms and made appropriate noises. Then Robertson took them outside. It was dusking over, with the sea a steady background murmur to a piping, squawking chorus from terns and gulls roosting along the cliff face.

91

'Here's what I reckon will interest you, Carrick.' Robertson led the way to the boathouse, heaved open a heavy sliding door, and stood back. 'Meet *Anna*.'

Resting on a rubber-tyred launching cradle, she was a slim twenty-foot sailing boat with a sleek, varnished hard chine hull. An alloy mast and spars were lashed neatly to the roof of the small day cabin.

'Sloop-rigged, three-foot draught and a self-draining cockpit,' said Robertson proudly. 'I got her as a trade-in against a new car last summer. Complete with a spare set of sails – and she'll work single-handed without a murmur.'

'Out there?' Mora frowned towards the sea. 'Isn't this a fairly dangerous coast for – for –'

'For an amateur?' Robertson shrugged. 'I'm strictly a fair-weather sailor. Anyway, the worst part is easing past that hog-back of rock. There's only one channel, which I've buoyed. Once outside, you're in open water.'

'She looks sturdy enough.' Carrick walked round the sloop, inspecting her with a keen professional eye. 'Done much sailing?'

'Some, down south.' Robertson stopped and frowned as his name was called. They went to the door and saw his wife beckoning from the house.

'Telephone, Harvey,' she called again. 'It's Kip, from the garage.'

Robertson swore under his breath. 'Wait here. I won't be long.'

He went off at a lumbering trot. Mora Atholl smiled at the sight then turned to Carrick. 'Well, what do you think of the layout?'

'I'd say he'd got everything going for him,' mused Carrick. 'But I get a feeling he's a little gritty on the marital side.'

'She doesn't seem to mind.' Mora ran a finger along the boat's smooth varnish. 'I had a talk with her this afternoon. She more or less admitted that every now and again he boils over and packs her off to "visit friends" for a couple of days.' Her lips tightened. 'A man wouldn't do that to me.'

'I can't imagine one wanting to,' murmured Carrick and saw her smile again. 'Let's have another look around before it gets really dark.'

They strolled down the slipway to the water's edge. Carrick saw a couple of dead fish lying further along but said nothing, watching Mora throw pebbles into the waves. Then heavy feet came crunching towards them.

'Sorry,' growled Robertson as he drew near. 'That damned fool foreman of mine won't take a decision on his own. He's working late on a job, stripping down an engine, and hit trouble – the kind that can cost money.' He peered at his watch in the gathering gloom. 'Time for another drink before you go, Carrick?'

'No thanks. But I want to say goodbye to your wife on the way.' As they started walking towards the house, Mora in the middle, Carrick tried to keep his manner casual. 'Did Andy have other friends around Quinbegg? I'm interested in what he did in his spare time.'

'Just interested?' Robertson slowed his pace, frowning. 'Carrick, I'm beginning to have an odd feeling about all of this. Whether – well, whether you people maybe know more about what happened than you're admitting.' He stopped. 'Was it an accident?'

Carrick faced him and shrugged, adopting a cautious but confidential air. 'That's one I wouldn't like to answer yet. We've found a few things that have us worried.' He paused for what he hoped was the right length of time. 'Let's say a lot will depend on what the technical people decide when they've seen the submersible.'

'Like that, eh?' Robertson's grunt of satisfaction faded as he glanced at Mora. 'Makes it worse for you, girl – and I'm sorry. Losing someone in an accident is bad enough, but –' He pursed his lips and shook his head. 'Anyway, let's see now – friends? No, I can't think of anyone else Jeffrey knew well around here. If I do remember later I'll certainly let you know.'

Carrick left it at that and stayed silent, conscious that it was costing Mora an effort to do the same. They reached the house, he said goodbye to Mrs Robertson, thanked her for her invitation to come again . . . and then he was back in the MG, headlamps cutting into the night as it growled away.

'Just what's scheduled when you get back that is so important?' asked Mora as they swung on to the main road.

'I didn't say there was anything special,' answered Carrick lazily, his mind lulled by the engine's steady purr.

'No.' It came with a frosty edge. 'You never tell people much. Unless you happen to want something in return.'

'It might look that way.' Carrick turned in his seat, studying the way the glow from the instrument lights shadowed her firm-lipped profile. 'All right, I plan on having a long talk with someone. Maybe "talk" is the wrong word. He won't welcome the idea.'

'Preacher?'

'He certainly matters,' admitted Carrick. 'But right now he should be busy with a string of lobster creels.'

Mora tapped the steering wheel with the fingers of one hand, her annoyance plain. 'Then is it one of the research officers, a man called Leslie?'

Carrick jerked upright, stared, then grabbed her by the arm. 'Pull up,' he said firmly.

The MG coasted to a halt with its nearside wheels on the grass verge. She switched off and waited.

94

'Why pick on Leslie?'

'Does it matter?' she parried almost maliciously.

He nodded grimly. 'It does – a lot, believe me.'

'It's only that I saw him this morning. At least, I think I –' She broke off and tried again. 'Webb, I didn't sleep much last night. Then in the morning I went for a walk down to the harbour, early on – before break-fast, in fact.' She shrugged uncertainly. 'I saw Preacher when I got to the outer basin. He was standing on the deck of an old boat and talking to another man. Then the man left him and walked towards the *Clavella*.'

'You said Leslie,' reminded Carrick. 'Had you met him before?'

'No. But – well, Mrs Robertson showed me some photographs this afternoon, colour pictures she's taken. They were in the mail waiting when she got back. A couple of them were snapshots of Andy at the house. Then I saw the same man in another picture and she said his name was Leslie, one of the research officers.' She drew a deep breath. 'And that's all. Satisfied?'

Carrick swore under his breath. 'Did you see Leslie give anything to Preacher?'

She shook her head, puzzled.

'I can try to find out,' said Carrick softly. 'Or to be accurate we can, beginning as soon as we get to Quinbegg.' He saw her frown and the question shaping on her lips. 'We'll start by making absolutely sure it was Leslie you saw this morning. That should be easy enough to settle, easier than what comes after if you're right.'

If Peter Leslie had been aboard Preacher's boat it hadn't been to discuss the weather, lobster fishing, or his state of health. And if Preacher still had those research papers the fact raised several nightmare possibilities.

* * *

He told part of the story on the way. Not all, but enough to satisfy her. Listening intently, she still concentrated equally on driving, giving a heel and toe performance between brake and accelerator which kept the MG at tyre-punishing pace and had Carrick anchoring himself to the passenger grab-handle.

Their speed eased once the first of Quinbegg's thin scatter of street lights showed ahead. But he was still glad when they jerked to a stop on the quayside near the *Clavella*'s gangway. Climbing out, he took Mora by the arm and started towards the gangway.

'Chief – hold on!' The shout came as their feet touched the dock. Sam Paxton hurried towards them, his face a struggle between relief and apprehension. 'He found you – well, thank the Lord for that much!'

'I wasn't lost.' Carrick had a sudden chill sense of disaster. 'What's the panic? Who was looking for me?'

The mate swallowed. 'I thought – Clapper Bell said –' He clawed his beard nervously. 'Sir, it's Leslie – he escaped. Knocked out his guard, dumped him in the cabin and got away.'

'How long ago?'

'I'm not sure. But it's about twenty minutes since we found the guard.'

'You've searched the ship?'

Paxton nodded miserably. 'He's ashore, sir.'

Carrick felt a wave of angry despair. 'How the hell did he get past the gangway watch?'

There were plenty of possible answers and they both knew it. Paxton shook his head. 'I don't know, sir. Clapper Bell and half the crew are ashore now, looking for him. We –' he hesitated – 'we had to get a doctor to tend the crewman. Sergeant MacKenzie came with him. They're both still aboard.'

Carrick almost groaned. Having the county police involved was a final touch of havoc. He thought fast, trying to cling to the priorities.

'Sam, get over to the outer basin – right now. If Preacher Noah's boat is out come straight back and tell me. If it isn't, stay there, watch it, but don't go aboard till I come.'

He turned to Mora. 'I've a petty officer wandering around the village – close-cut fair hair, over six feet, built like a bull. Can you try to find him and tell him I'm back?'

She nodded without argument. 'I'll take the car.'

He left them to it and hurried below, instinctively heading for the research area, coming to a grim-faced halt as he entered the main laboratory.

One of the benches had been cleared of equipment and was being used as a makeshift blanket-covered surgery table. Bending over it, a mild-faced stranger in a sports jacket and sweater was adjusting the final layers in a positive turban of bandages round the head of an engine-room greaser. The man lay very still, his eyes closed. Beside them, the scowl on Sergeant Mac-Kenzie's face instantly deepened.

'Another o' your unfortunate accidents, chief officer?' he queried acidly. 'What's the story you're going to tell this time?'

Ignoring him, Carrick turned to the doctor. 'How is he?'

'Lucky,' said the doctor with minimal concern. 'He took a bash that could have fractured his skull, but it must be made of boiler steel. I've stitched a gash, given him something to kill the pain, and all he'll have by morning is a headache like a three-day hangover.' He poked the greaser with a firm forefinger. 'Right, laddie?'

The man groaned and tried to nod.

'I've got the story,' growled Sergeant MacKenzie. 'He heard moaning noises coming from Leslie's cabin, thought he'd better check, looked in, and was clubbed. Here's what did it.' He showed a long,

97

heavy, rubber-sealed torch. 'And it makes a damned good substitute for a cosh. Now your turn, chief officer. What's this all about?'

'I could say that was ship's business,' said Carrick with little conviction.

'Like hell,' snarled MacKenzie, looking again at the greaser. 'That bash on the skull comes close to attempted murder. At very least it amounts to serious assault.' He growled to himself. 'The mate admits Leslie is ashore and you can't find him. Which means he's loose in my parish – and I'm running no risk of Quinbegg folk being attacked.'

'It isn't likely,' said Carrick patiently, then sighed. 'All right, sergeant – you want the story. Here's as much as you'll get from me, and I'm spelling it out. Leslie was confined under guard on my orders. He was being held for interrogation pending Commander Dobie's return tomorrow. The matter concerned is covered by the Official Secrets Act. And that's your lot.'

'A load o' blasted rubbish,' rasped MacKenzie. Then, as he saw Carrick's expression, his face gradually lost some of its ruddy hue. 'God, I think you mean it!'

'I mean it and we're wasting time,' snapped Carrick. 'I've an idea where he might be – and that's on Preacher's boat if it is still in the basin.'

MacKenzie's jaw sagged then he nodded. 'Why stand here then? Doc, wait for me. I'll be back.'

From the *Clavella*'s berth to the outer basin was a short sprint under the pale, clouded moonlight. The quayside was deserted, the crews from the fishing boats probably snug in the bar at the Corrie Arms or similarly engaged. As they reached their goal Sam Paxton stepped from the shadow of some stacked crates.

'The boat's still here, sir – haven't seen anyone come near it,' he reported eagerly. 'But there's no sign of a light aboard.'

'Then we'll find out.' Carrick led the way down the iron wall-ladder, dropped lightly to the lifeboat's deck, and headed for the cabin door. Behind him, Sergeant MacKenzie landed on the boards with a heavy thud. Carrick turned to scowl then froze as an urgent thumping sound began from the other side of the door. Grabbing the handle he turned and pulled. The door didn't budge.

'Locked?' MacKenzie pushed beside him, peered briefly, then gestured both Fishery men back. 'My department –' He took a half-step away and kicked, the heel of his police issue boot taking the wood with explosive force just below the lock in a way which made even the frame quiver. 'Try now.'

The door didn't so much open as fall loose on what was left of its hinges. Carrick went through, stumbling down a couple of steps into pitch darkness. A muffled, gobbling noise and a renewed thumping greeted him then Sam Paxton was shining a torch and the beam showed Preacher Noah glaring apoplectically from the only bunk. He was on his back, in his shirt sleeves, his mouth was gagged, and his feet and hands had been lashed together with heavy cord.

A kerosene lamp hung from the roof. Carrick used his cigarette lighter to get it going then turned as the warm light filled the cabin. Sawing with a pocket knife, Sergeant MacKenzie already had the cord cut from Preacher's feet. His hands were freed next then, as the gag came loose, he spat it out with a roar of rage.

'Where is the damned heathen? If you've got him I'll –'

'Simmer down,' said MacKenzie, with a gruff relief.

'You sound in one piece and that's what matters. Take it easy for a minute.'

'Take it easy?' Preacher took no comfort from the words. His angular, bristled face twisted wrathfully in the lamplight. 'Man, even if I sin in the doing of it I'll square accounts with that ungrateful devil!'

'Was it Leslie?' asked Carrick bluntly.

'Aye.' The pale blue eyes met his and for once wavered. 'He belted me on the head when my back was turned.'

'How long since he left?'

The thin shoulders shrugged. 'Twenty minutes maybe. Ach, I couldn't be sure. All I know is I woke up in the dark, trussed like a hen.'

Carrick nodded. 'And he got what he came for?'

Preacher's sigh was sufficient answer.

'Then he's on his way.' Carrick chewed his lip. 'But he'll need transport to get clear, either car or boat. The only way to stop him now is a general alert – your side, sergeant.'

'Just like that?' MacKenzie raised a stubborn eyebrow. 'I still want to know what the hell he's done.'

'You called it serious assault,' said Carrick curtly. 'Won't that do for a start?'

'Aye.' MacKenzie nodded reluctantly, almost angrily. 'I'll get the word out. Sir.' The last word held its own bitterness. He spun on his heel and clumped out.

Carrick sighed and beckoned Sam Paxton closer. 'You'd better head back to the *Clavella*. Get the doctor to come over here when he's finished.'

'For me?' Preacher shook a shaggy, determined head. 'No, I'm all right. I need no doctor. There's some brandy in thon locker behind the door.' He paused then emphasized heavily, 'Medicinal brandy. If –'

Smothering a grin Sam Paxton found the bottle, slopped a generous measure into a tin cup, and handed it over. Preacher swallowed the amber spirit with a theatrical show of distaste, accepted a refill and gave a repeat performance. But he pushed away the next offer. 'Enough. Put it away. Any more would be for pleasure, and alcohol should not be enjoyed – only used.'

Shrugging, Paxton returned the bottle.

'I'll cope now, Sam,' said Carrick. 'Head back and keep an eye on things.'

Reluctantly, the mate obeyed. Carrick stood for a moment, looking round the cabin. It was furnished in spartan style, the bunk bedding thin and patched, paint peeling from most of the fitments and roof, bared metal rusting. Beyond the essentials there was only a shelf of books, their covers frayed and mildewed.

'And now the questions, eh?' Preacher was sitting up, legs over the side of the bunk, face calm but resigned.

'Some of them,' agreed Carrick, staying where he was. 'Did you know what was in those papers?'

'I looked,' confessed Preacher, mild shame in his voice.

'And understood enough to have doubts about what the skippers' meeting should do?'

A faint smile and a nod was his answer.

Carrick shoved his cap back on his head and sighed. 'I know he brought them here this morning. But why to you?'

'Maybe because I was nearest and he was in a bit o' a panic.' Preacher shrugged expressively. 'He told me he was on the fishermen's side, that the package held information which would tell the world what the *Clavella* had really been doin'. All he wanted was for me to keep it safe till he came for it again.'

'But you looked,' said Carrick.

Preacher smiled self-consciously. 'Well, the kettle was steaming and the envelope wasn't too well stuck down. Wouldn't any reasonable man want to know what he'd been asked to look after?'

Shaking his head, Carrick didn't try to answer. 'How much of it did make sense, Preacher?'

'Enough for me to know there's some kind o' microscopic life out in the Minch that's a killer – and that the *Clavella* people are making it into something worse.'

'Only in a test tube, looking for answers,' continued Carrick swiftly.

'So the notes said,' agreed Preacher unperturbed. 'But when man interferes wi' nature on his own head be it.'

'Your head mainly, so far,' said Carrick with a forced attempt at humour. 'What happened when Leslie came this evening?'

Preacher scratched his chin, frowning at the memory. 'Well, he arrived looking like he'd been swimming part o' the way – soaking wet and shivering like he'd fall down. According to him, he just wanted his package and the chance to get away – that he knew where to take it.' He shrugged again. 'Well, I had the package under the mattress here and bent down to fetch it out. When I did, he hit me.' Gently, he touched the back of his head. 'Now why should he do that, eh?'

'Maybe because you started to argue with him,' said Carrick softly. 'Am I right?'

'I'd a mind to keep some of the stuff,' admitted Preacher uneasily. 'What you might call a bit o' insurance. But –' he sighed, grunted up from the bunk, ran a hand under the mattress and shook his head – 'it's gone now. All of it, even the film.'

'What film?' Startled, Carrick took a quick step nearer.

'Two reels o' cine film, still unprocessed.' Preacher looked at him with equal surprise. 'Man, don't you even know what you're after?'

'I know less by the moment,' grated Carrick. 'Or it seems that way.'

Preacher sniffed. 'Well, I've nothing more anyway. And I should be out wi' those lobster creels –'

'You go nowhere,' Carrick told him bluntly. 'Try it, and you'll land in one of MacKenzie's cells. That's a promise.'

'Then I'll be sending Fishery Protection a bill for two dozen lobsters that didn't get caught,' retorted Preacher blithely. 'Anything to stop me going on deck for a breath o' air?'

'No, but I'll be right behind you.'

'Law and order can be a fine thing,' said Preacher sardonically, pulling on his jacket. 'I get hit on the head two nights running – and the only result is I've to say "please" before I can move on my own boat.'

Still muttering, he walked shakily across the cabin, mounted the steps, opened the door, and stood framed in the cabin light for a moment.

The whipcrack of the shot and the slamming impact of bullet on wood came almost together. Splinters flew, Carrick heard a high-pitched yelp of pain – then he tackled Preacher by the knees, dragging him back while a second shot smashed against the door frame. He left the thin figure tumbled unceremoniously on the deck and quickly extinguished the kerosene lamp.

Another shot cracked out. A metal cooking pot on one of the shelves jumped and clanged. Preacher tried to struggle to his feet and Carrick shoved him down again.

'Stay there, you idiot!' Ignoring the man's protests he crouched his way back to the steps, tensed, then threw himself out of the opened door and rolled across the cockpit. As he crouched down again he

103

spotted a pin-flash of light from the far side of the basin as the fourth shot blasted. Splinters flew from the lifeboat's gunwale, the aim wilder than before.

Shouts and the swift clatter of running feet showed the shooting had attracted plenty of attention. Taking a chance, Carrick sprang for the iron ladder, scrambled to the top, and stared across the basin.

The dim moonlight showed a vague, shadow-like figure running – a figure already too far away for there to be any sense in going after it. He watched till it vanished into the night – and moments later a hustle of fishermen arrived, two of the *Clavella*'s ratings with them, Sam Paxton not far behind.

'Anyone hurt?' demanded the man in the lead, a husky, scar-faced fisherman with one fist wrapped round the shaft of a gutting knife. 'Where's Preacher?'

'Safe and sound,' assured Carrick blandly.

The man scowled suspiciously. 'We heard shots, mister.'

'Heard them?' Carrick grinned. 'Any nearer and I'd have thought my name was on them. That was pretty wild target practice.'

The cluster of faces remained unconvinced, openly sceptical.

'What's a Fishery snoop doing on Preacher's boat?' growled a voice from the rear.

'Just visiting,' assured Carrick. He looked down, saw Preacher emerging from the cabin, and raised his voice. 'They're worried about you.'

'I'm glad somebody is,' said Preacher gloomily. 'All right, lads – everything's fine. It was just a fool wi' a gun, like he says. Someone trying to scare me for a laugh, I suppose.'

The scar-faced fisherman hesitated. 'Maybe if we went looking –' he began.

'He's far away by now,' said Preacher shortly. 'I'll tell the police later. Forget it. Away back to your beer.'

The cluster dispersed, still muttering among themselves. Carrick signalled Paxton and the two ratings to stay then called softly down to Preacher.

'Thanks for playing along.'

'Don't bother,' said Preacher flatly. 'If he's still out there I'm not risking a Quinbegg man walking into his gun. That's all.'

'Our worry,' agreed Carrick mildly. He turned to the ratings. 'The mate and I have a little job to do. I want this boat here when we get back. And don't let Preacher wander.'

Ignoring the rumbling protest from below, he led Paxton away from the boat at a deliberate, strolling pace. The mate fought down his curiosity as long as he could then gave in.

'Sir – what did happen?'

'Target practice, like I said,' replied Carrick laconically. 'Except that Preacher was meant to be bullseye.'

He heard Paxton suck a startled breath, grinned and continued the same apparently casual pace round the basin. When he reached his destination, the spot where he'd seen that pin-flash which had to have come from a gun's muzzle, he found it was the site of a small, derelict brick hut with an empty doorway.

'Still got your torch?'

'Here, sir.' Paxton played the beam into the black interior and across the rough concrete floor. It glinted on three brass cartridge cases lying almost side by side then found the fourth where it had rolled into a corner. They went in, Paxton brought the torch beam close to the nearest cartridge, then he frowned over it and whistled.

'Target practice is right, sir,' he said uneasily. 'They're rifle calibre, .300.'

'Expert knowledge?' murmured Carrick.

Paxton grinned weakly. 'Ever gone deerstalking, sir? I did once, not far from here. And I saw a stag clobbered at half a mile with a .300 – in one side, out the other, clean as a whistle.'

'Nice to know.' Carefully, using a pencil tip and his handkerchief, Carrick gathered the cartridges. They could collect the bullets from Preacher's boat – but whether the result would help he doubted. Poaching a deer from the hills was a routine part of stocking up the winter larder in the north-west. He wondered just how many unlicensed rifles were hidden within half an hour's drive of Quinbegg. 'Anything else?'

They drew a blank and tried outside. Behind the hut a dark, empty lane led along the side of a blank-walled warehouse shed. Giving up, they returned to the hut. As they reached it Paxton gulped and pointed at a bulky shape lounging in the doorway.

'Just me.' Clapper Bell eased from the shadows, grinning. 'I knew you were somewhere around – thought I might as well wait.'

'You gave the mate palpitations,' said Carrick dryly. 'Any word of Leslie being seen?'

'Not as much as a sniff.' Bell shook his head sadly. 'We went through Quinbegg from one end to the other – not that it takes very long. Then I heard about the shooting an' decided to come over. Eh . . . think it was Leslie pulling the trigger?'

'It wouldn't make much sense,' said Carrick slowly, puzzling over that one himself. 'He could have killed Preacher without any fuss before he left the boat, so why wait till later?'

'Maybe he was trying to nail you,' said the bo'sun pointedly.

'Then he has damned bad eyesight. Preacher was in the cabin doorway with plenty of light behind him – and we certainly don't rate as twins.' Carrick took the cigarette Bell offered, accepted a light, and drew on the smoke. 'Did you meet up with Mora Atholl?'

106

'Not long before the target practice. When we found out what happened she said she'd look in on Preacher.' Bell saw Carrick's eyebrows rise and shrugged. 'Her kind aren't easy to stop when they make up their minds about something.'

Carrick smiled wryly, hefted the little package of cartridges, then gave them to Paxton. 'Sam, another job for you. Find Sergeant MacKenzie and give him these as a peace-offering. Then keep him occupied any way you can – but keep him away from Preacher's boat till I've had another try there. Better go with him, Clapper. If everything's fairly peaceful you can take a wander up the village later and plug into the gossip network. They should have plenty to talk about after this lot.'

He watched them leave, smoked the cigarette for about half its length, then flicked it away and walked towards the basin. The moonlight made him a clear, conspicuous target but somehow he knew that didn't matter.

No, it couldn't have been Leslie behind that rifle. Which meant the situation came right back to a deadlier version of what had happened to Preacher the previous night. Yet why should anyone want to try to kill the tall, lean eccentric? Before, the motive might have been the simple one of creating trouble and a diversion. Now it could be a lot deeper.

The main truth hurt. So far he didn't know anything that particularly mattered. Until he did, his adversary was prepared to treat him with something close to contempt.

Preacher Noah had the kettle boiling on his cabin's small coal stove. An adhesive dressing covered the gash a splinter had raked across his forehead and apart from a nod he almost ignored Carrick's return while he concentrated on instructing Mora Atholl on the higher mysteries of tea-making.

'It's an art, a science on its own,' he said with a ponderous solemnity. 'You begin with matching the best blend o' tea to the character of the local water. Tea like this –' he tapped a battered old caddy which bore a picture of Queen Victoria with the nose chipped off – 'real stuff, none o' that paper bag road-sweepings nonsense they use in the cities.'

Mora smiled in response and gave Carrick a fractional wink as he sat beside her on the bunk.

'Warm the pot first – most folk do that.' Preacher poured a dash of boiling water into a stained teapot, swirled it round, then emptied it into the galley basin. 'Then the tea goes in – not too little, not too much.' A fist descended into the caddy, emerged clutching a massive quantity of black leaves, and dumped them in the pot. 'Now the bit that really matters. Never take the kettle to the pot, always the pot to the kettle, and that way you're using really boiling water, which makes all the difference.' Triumphantly, he matched actions to words, filled the pot, dropped its lid in place, and set it aside. 'Then allow two minutes to infuse and always discard the first spoutful. Got it all, lassie?'

'I think so,' she agreed mildly.

'Good.' Gripping the lapels of his black jacket, he switched his attention to Carrick. 'Before you say it, chief officer, I'm in your debt again. That's getting to be a habit.'

'And embarrassing for you,' said Carrick with a touch of sarcasm. 'Any sense in asking who was behind that rifle?'

'None, because I've no idea. But he'll have his own trial and judgment.' As the man spoke he dumped a trio of tin cups on the table, added a bag of sugar, a spoon and a sticky tin of condensed milk, then stepped back satisfied. 'We all meet judgement.'

'Some quicker than others,' said Mora quietly.

'Aye.' Preacher frowned at her. 'How much of all this does she know, Carrick?'

'Enough to know she can't talk about it outside. The same applies to you.'

Preacher's answer was a derisive grunt. 'You have my word on it – but only for now. Anything else?'

Carrick nodded. 'Captain Jeffrey came to see you a few days ago. I'd like to hear more of what you talked about – not just the part about him asking you to give him more time.'

'He knows why,' said Mora. Leaning forward, dark hair glinting in the soft light of the kerosene lamp, she moistened her lips. 'Webb, I felt he had to realize that what happened to Andy was no accident. It seemed to make sense, for his own good as much as anything else.'

'More sense than I've had from any man around here,' growled Preacher. He nursed the teapot with one hand. 'Captain Jeffrey asked me to keep my silence about this, and I gave my word. But if what the girl says is right –'

'It is,' nodded Carrick. 'What happened was murder.'

The thin, stubbled cheeks sucked together in sad distaste. 'Then you'd better hear the truth of it. Captain Jeffrey wanted information about foreign trawlers. Where we sighted them, when, how often. I told him what I could, then – well, he went on from there.'

'About what?' Carrick wondered if anything short of a bomb could hurry the lean figure opposite.

'He asked if the local boats ever caught sight o' a submarine in these parts, particularly around the Quinbegg Trench,' said Preacher in a calm, undramatic voice. 'Well, nobody ever fishes up that way –

it never was worth while. But there's been a story or two from folk who've passed there by night.'

'That they'd seen submarines?'

'So they say.' Calmly, Preacher turned and lifted the teapot. 'You'll have a cup before you go?'

Carrick nodded dumbly and he began pouring.

Chapter Six

Shafts of pale morning sunlight struck through the *Clavella's* wardroom portholes, one landing exactly on Commander Dobie's head and shoulders to frame him like a wayward halo. He sat at the table, briefcase in front of him, a cigarette burning unheeded between his fingers.

'They're not ours, not American, not NATO.' Voice quiet and flat, he gave a fractional shake of his head. 'People a lot higher than Department level have checked all possible submarine movements, with negative answers. You know what that leaves.'

Seated opposite, Webb Carrick nodded silently. A lot had happened in the night which had passed. But apart from the m.f.v.'s radio stuttering a long series of coded signals little of the activity had been around Quinbegg. Nor had the basic situation changed. Despite a full-scale alert which had spread far beyond county boundaries there was still no trace of Peter Leslie. And now Dobie was back, delivered again by helicopter ... a man who seemed to have aged beyond belief in the space of these few hours.

'As for the trawlers –' Dobie laid a weary hand on the briefcase – 'we thought we knew all about them. The navy keep their tabs on the electronic warehouses and we're left with the ordinary workboats.'

Carrick knew what he meant. The Iron Curtain countries were signatories to the new North East

Atlantic Convention, accepting the same international fishing codes, recognizing the powers of any nation's fishery protection squadron and its rights to have local jurisdiction over foreign vessels. It was international policing. So far it had worked smoothly.

'We thought,' repeated Dobie bitterly. 'Well, now we know we were wrong. I've had every coastal sighting report of an East Europe trawler analysed, going back over the last six months. Ninety per cent didn't matter. But the rest included a fairly steady trickle of vessels heading into the Minch, hanging around for a couple of days without doing anything, then easing back out into the Atlantic.'

'Shelter or repairs,' murmured Carrick. 'They could claim one or other, I suppose – and it would be hard to prove them wrong. Like now, for instance.'

Quinbegg's weather prophets had beaten the official Meteorological Office forecast by several hours. But the eight a.m. shipping forecast had finally caught up. Severe south-westerly gales, reaching Force Ten, were expected to reach the Minch area within the next twelve hours.

'It doesn't much matter either way. As long as they don't fish or break customs regulations what they do is officially none of our damned business.' Dobie scowled at his cigarette and stubbed it with a vicious deliberation.

'So much of the seafire data disappearing with Leslie is one kind of disaster. But this new submarine business rates right up beside it in terms of trouble.'

'Andy really had his teeth into something,' mused Carrick.

'Even with Humbey to help, Andy Jeffrey was a damned fool to go it alone,' rasped Dobie. He shut his eyes briefly, took a deep breath, then looked up. 'Got those research bods handy?'

'They're outside, sir.' Exactly why they should be wanted puzzled Carrick. But among the overnight signals had been one which authorized a minimal briefing to Haydock and Allison and ordered them to remain available.

'Bring them in.'

Carrick obeyed. Unusually spick and span from clean white shirts to highly polished shoes, the two junior research officers entered warily, mumbled a greeting and were gestured into chairs.

'You're here for one reason only,' said Dobie bluntly. 'Peter Leslie's speciality was thermal studies and tidal patterns. Both of you assisted him from time to time?'

They nodded in unison.

'Did he ever complain, object or make any kind of comment about that work?'

The two juniors exchanged glances. Jim Haydock did the answering. 'He griped now and again, sir. Went on about it being one stage short of scientific prostitution. We – well, we didn't pay much attention to him when he was in that kind of mood.'

'He dropped the same kind of hint to Chief Officer Carrick last night – not long before he made what we'll call an embarrassing exit.' Pursing his lips, Dobie stayed silent for a moment. 'I know what he meant. Carrick doesn't. Do you?'

By some tacit agreement it was Allison's turn. He eased his spectacles a fraction higher and cleared his throat.

'Undersea forecasting, sir. That and oceanographic mapping.'

Dobie nodded approvingly. 'Explain.'

'In plain language?' Allison caught a warning glitter flicker in Dobie's eyes and hurried on. 'Well, when you've different water layers at sea – things like thermal differences, salinity, tidal current factors – you can work out where particularly rough weather may

113

happen. Or where there's likely to be a good fishing area. But – uh – the same factors can be pretty important to the navy in terms of sonar detection. Sonar's principle is a sound wave which goes down till it strikes an object then echoes back. Things like sandwich layers of water or salinity variations refract the sonar waves.'

'So if you were a submarine commander and wanted to hide your vessel?' rapped his inquisitor.

Allison answered without hesitation. 'I'd check my stream charts and undersea forecast information and duck under the nearest thermal layer.'

'And how would you rate conditions out around the Quinbegg Trench?'

The research juniors exchanged another glance.

'Ideal for it, sir,' confirmed Haydock. 'Get down there, sit snug on the bottom, and you'd never be found.'

'Wait a bit.' Frowning, Carrick leaned forward. 'We located the submersible by echo-sounder, and inside the Trench. How do you explain that away?'

Haydock permitted himself the beginnings of a smile. 'We were working from a fixed marker, we were near the edge of the Trench where the effects were lessened – and *Clavella*'s research equipment is pretty sophisticated, sir.'

'Right.' Commander Dobie built a slow, sardonic steeple with his fingertips. 'Now I'll complete your education, Carrick. Forecasts of world-wide underwater conditions are constantly provided to all NATO patrol submarines and particularly to all British and American nuclear submarines. British reports emanate from Western Fleet headquarters at Northwood. The Americans have similar arrangements based on their Navy Hydrographic Office at Washington.'

'Pooled information?' asked Carrick, conscious of a pattern being gradually woven.

'Naturally – we've all got budget troubles,' said Dobie dryly. 'And there's a hell of a lot of work involved. Someday it will be done by satellites fitted with infra-red sensors. But right now it comes down to heaving fairly expensive one-trip gadgets called – ah –'

'Bathythermographs,' offered Allison helpfully.

'Exactly.' Dobie gave a grunt of thanks. 'These – ah – things are heaved over the side. They transmit temperature readings and other data as they sink. Everyone is in on the act – research ships, weather ships, the US Coastguard, aircraft, even a few merchant shipping lines.'

Carrick looked down at the polished table-top, his mouth tightening a little. 'So Leslie was right – he was being used for a lot more than fishery research?'

'Indirectly, yes.' Dobie almost snarled the words. 'Damn it, nobody can live in a private little ivory tower and any research has its by-products. If you won't use them the other fellow will. It works both ways – space research produced the non-stick frying pan, fishery research helps turn up where a submarine can hide. Anybody's submarine.' He stopped and glanced pointedly at Allison and Haydock. 'That's it for now. You say nothing and you heard nothing. Understood?'

They mumbled agreement and left. As the door closed behind them Dobie relaxed back with a sigh. 'Good records and they've been vetted. No worries there. Well, Carrick, put it together.'

He didn't rush his answer. 'Some of the Iron Curtain trawlers are taking routine data forecasts on the Quinbegg Trench. As long as Soviet submarines know conditions are ripe they can come in, lie undetected and –' he hesitated but was encouraged on by Dobie's nod – 'and maybe surface by night to rendezvous with other trawlers.'

115

'To stock up on supplies, relieve personnel, any- thing like that,' agreed Dobie. 'That's the top brass theory, the reason why they've pushed the panic but- ton. A nuclear boat's patrol endurance is limited by the human and stores factor – not the mechanical side. Calculate the time saved if a Soviet submarine on, say, South Atlantic patrol doesn't have to make the final round trip leg to one of their Baltic bases and you boost that patrol potential by maybe ten per cent.'

Carrick nodded. It could be put in an even more simple way. It meant the equivalent of a ten per cent increase in ready, deployed missile power.

'There are bound to be places like this in other parts of the world.' Dobie shoved back his chair, crossed to the porthole, and stared out at the sunlight. 'Well, we don't know how much Andy Jeffrey had put together, and the film in the submersible's camera didn't help – it was ruined. But I can guess what was on the cine footage Leslie grabbed. Something big and grey snoozing on the seabed with a dirty great hammer and sickle on its welcome mat.'

'I wonder who got the biggest fright,' murmured Carrick.

'Obviously there's a Soviet agent operating on shore,' went on Dobie, ignoring the interruption. 'One with a radio link – and he received orders to dispose of the submersible double-quick. To me that means the submarine commander wasn't sure if he'd been spotted, and there the way Jeffrey acted did help – or does now.' He sighed almost despondently. 'Once upon a time the navy would simply have sent a couple of destroyers out to drop a string of depth charges along the Trench as a "practice exercise". But not these days. We're too damned polite – or scared.'

Carrick barely heard him. He was thinking of Peter Leslie, wondering if the research officer was shivering somewhere up among the cold, bleak hills, probably still clutching that vital seafire package. The information it contained still seemed more frightening in potential than the threat posed by even a flotilla of nuclear submarines.

'Now Leslie is different. My guess and hope is that he started off as completely separate.' Not for the first time the Chief Superintendent of Fisheries showed a fantastic mind-reading ability. 'The fact that he has the bad luck to have a conscience and sees things in a special way was just chance having a sick joke in the middle of the rest.' He sighed heavily. 'But what terrifies me now is if he eventually set up any kind of contact with the opposition.'

'He told Preacher he knew where to take the stuff,' said Carrick gravely.

'If he meant it that way, they'll ferry him out of here express delivery.' Dobie spun on his heel and glared across the wardroom. 'Well, God help us, we've got what I was fool enough to want before. We're on our own.'

Carrick stared at him. 'But the security squads –'

'Couldn't stick their noses into a place like Quinbegg without being spotted straight off,' rasped Dobie. 'They've sealed off Quinbegg on the landward side and guarantee it. Roads blocked, every hill path patrolled. But the rest is our headache, because we're already an accepted part of the scenery.'

'What about the police?'

'Under orders to co-operate and keep their mouths shut,' said Dobie. 'But again no extra men to be moved in. Everything must stay as normal and natural as possible. About the only thing I have been able to do is to move two of our fishery cruisers north – *Marlin*, which should make you happy, and *Skua*. They're looking for this Russian trawler, sighting report only. I don't want her skipper scared off, not till the top brass in London make up their tiny minds about what to do next.' He lit a cigarette and drew hungrily on the smoke. 'Which brings us down to a couple of people we can't control, Preacher and the Atholl girl.'

'Preacher's no problem.' Carrick quirked a grin. 'He went out lobstering at dawn with Clapper Bell along to hold his hand.' And there had been a guard on the boat all night.

'Good.' Dobie relaxed a little. 'The girl?'

'I'm seeing her this morning, away from the Robertson place. She went back there for the night but she knew how much to tell them ... just what the whole village knows. That Leslie went berserk for some reason, thumped one of our men, then attacked Preacher as he escaped.'

Dobie grunted. 'All right. Any loose ends?'

'A few, sir.' One of them involved an idea still shaping in his mind. 'But I'm working on them.'

'Well, don't try to do an Andy Jeffrey,' warned Dobie grimly. 'I've had my fill of dead heroes.' He collected his briefcase and started for the door. 'I'm going to make quite sure Sergeant MacKenzie knows how to behave, then make some phone calls. When Clapper Bell shows up, send him along. I may need him.'

'The Quinbegg skippers are meeting again today,' mused Carrick.

'Damn the skippers,' said Dobie.

The wardroom seemed an oddly peaceful place once he'd gone.

The skippers' meeting was scheduled for eleven a.m. Carrick watched them leave their boats, solitary, slightly embarrassed men in jerseys and seaboots, who brightened as they found company then headed in twos and threes towards the village. As the last went ashore Preacher Noah's boat spluttered in, heading for the outer basin.

He'd expected that too. Preacher wasn't likely to miss an audience. But Carrick didn't find himself worrying about how much the man would say. He had given his word and in his case that seemed enough.

Another five minutes passed. He was on deck, enjoying the sunlight but sheltered from the wind by the superstructure, when Clapper Bell returned over the gangway. The bo'sun had a slopping, water-filled bucket in one hand and gave a cheerful salute with the other.

'From Preacher,' grinned Bell, dumping the bucket at his feet. Two prime, angry lobsters wriggled in its depths. 'With compliments – he's in a good mood.'

'Then he's in a minority,' said Carrick absently. 'Any problems while you were with him?'

Bell shook his head. 'Only when he started singin' hymn tunes an' made me join in.'

'I've heard you on your own. That would be bad enough.' Carrick glanced round, saw hopeful eyes watching from the engine-room companionway and smiled slightly. 'Well, after a nice peaceful start to the day you won't object to a little work. And I don't mean bellying up to the bar at the Corrie Arms with Willie Dewar. Commander Dobie wants you at the police office.'

The bo'sun's grin faded. 'After me being stuck out on that flamin' boat since dawn?'

'Sergeant MacKenzie probably has a teabreak sometime,' said Carrick solemnly. 'Better move, Clapper. Leave your little friends at the galley on the way.'

Muttering under his breath, Bell trudged off with his bucket.

Work of his own ahead, Carrick took a last turn round the deck then went ashore and headed straight for the car park. The Department station wagon's engine fired at the first turn of the key and he set it moving, driving through the village and turning on to the main road north. He steered thoughtfully, mind back on the same almost impossible prospect which had dogged him most of the morning.

Peter Leslie and the Robertsons. A social call, a photograph and a dumpy little woman whose husband seemed to give her a rough time. But Eleanor Robertson believed in a cause, the kind of cause which rated her as at least on the same wavelength as the missing research officer.

Harvey Robertson ... that was the bit that didn't figure; he'd been the one who'd mocked his wife's 'brotherhood of man' ideas. Because he hadn't realized the significance behind what he was saying? Carrick chewed his lip, remembering the telephone call which had come in when they'd been at the house.

From the garage, according to the Robertsons. He wondered, knowing there was something he had missed, something nudging away at the back of his mind, eager to click into place.

If it got the chance. Changing gear for the hill at the end of the village, he reached at least a part decision. He would ask Dobie to arrange a check on the Robertsons' background.

The result might hold the answer to another puzzle. Why hadn't Andy Jeffrey gone to Robertson, in his auxiliary coastguard role, for information about submarine sightings?

Unless he had. Whistling tunelessly, he mulled that one over for a spell. The possibilities were there all right. Maybe it wasn't such a crazy notion.

Sticking to the main road, Carrick passed the turn-off which led to the Robertson house and drove another quarter mile through the bleak wind-swept coastal scenery. Then he brightened and took his foot off the accelerator as Mora appeared ahead. He stopped and she scrambled gratefully into the passenger seat, slamming the door the moment she was aboard.

'I'm frozen,' she complained, shivering. 'You said eleven o'clock.'

'Sorry, but –'

'Excuses can wait till I thaw out.' Mora rubbed her hands together then loosened the anorak jacket. She was in the outfit she'd worn when they'd first met, but with a heavy dark sweater added. 'Just keep that heater going – and tell me why you couldn't have picked me up at the Robertsons' place. That woman thought I was mad when I said I was going a walk.'

'Exercise never hurt anyone,' said Carrick mildly, setting the station wagon moving again. 'It's good for the figure – you don't want to get fat, do you?'

'And to hell with you, too,' she said frostily.

Half a mile on, the road curved as it passed an abandoned, roofless cottage. Slowing, he steered the vehicle over the verge and across a patch of one-time garden then stopped behind the old stone walls. They were hidden from the road. Rusted beer cans and a scattering of rubbish showed the place was a regular picnic spot for summer tourists. The view was out to sea, a sea which had changed its mood and even in sunlight had become a grey and featureless expanse.

Switching off, he sat back. 'There's a good reason for meeting like this, Mora. Even better than when I suggested it, when I was just being cautious. Now – well, the Robertsons could be involved.'

She stared at him. 'You've got to be joking.'

'Have I?' He offered her a cigarette, snapped his lighter, and her fingers touched his hand as she automatically shielded the tiny flame. 'What happened when you got back last night?'

'They already knew about Leslie. All the way out I rehearsed my little speech – but Robertson had been in the village anyway. His foreman telephoned again after we left and he had to go to the garage.' She grimaced at the memory. 'He'd heard all about it on the village grapevine, which ruined my entrance. But – look, you can't be serious!'

He shrugged and lit his own cigarette. 'How did his wife react to it all?'

'Upset, I suppose. But she didn't say much. It was Robertson who did the talking.'

'No more mention of Leslie visiting them?'

Mora shook her head. 'Not while I was around, anyway. But Eleanor did say she was tired and went to bed early. Robertson went down to the boatshed to work on his yacht for a spell – I didn't stay up for long, so I don't know when he got back. Everything seemed normal enough. Why?'

'Because of a few pretty limp possibilities and not much more,' admitted Carrick, drawing on his cigarette. 'But they're about all we've got right now. If I'm wrong – well, there are no medals going for mistakes on this job.'

She didn't answer, staring at him.

'Something wrong?' he asked, puzzled.

'No, not wrong.' She moistened her lips. 'It's what you said.'

'About the Robertsons?'

'About medals.' Mora faced him earnestly. 'Andy talked about medals too – that's the thing I've been trying to remember. It was the last time he phoned, Webb. He said he was going to try something new, that he'd either end up with a medal or in jail and that he wouldn't bet which way things would go.'

'And that was all?'

She nodded. 'I asked him what he meant. But he just laughed and said I'd hear soon enough. It – well, it didn't seem important, almost a joke at the time. In fact, maybe that's all it was anyway.'

'A medal or in jail . . .' Carrick murmured the words then his expression changed. Suddenly he reached over, put his hands on her shoulders, and kissed her firmly on the lips. Grinning, he let her go. 'That's what we needed!'

Flushed, still bewildered, she drew back with a slight frown. 'Meaning what?'

'He said "a medal or in jail",' repeated Carrick. 'Now exactly when did he call you?'

'Four days ago, early in the evening.'

He nodded, satisfied. 'And that same evening someone broke into Harvey Robertson's garage. Broke in and left again without taking anything that mattered.'

Her mouth fell open. 'Andy?'

'I think so. It certainly fits.' Carrick tapped a hand on the steering wheel for emphasis. 'First, by then we've worked out he knew the Quinbegg Trench was being used by submarines. Second, he'd probably realized that they were also in contact with an agent ashore. Which in turn meant a radio link, with a transmitter located somewhere in the village.'

'So he went looking in the garage but couldn't find anything there?' She considered carefully then nodded a reluctant agreement. 'I suppose it's possible.'

'It fits, Mora.' Winding down his window, Carrick flicked the rest of his cigarette over towards the beer cans.

'And so does the next piece. The very next day Eleanor Robertson was packed off to visit her friends again. Once he'd got her out of the way Robertson had no home ties to worry about, nobody to ask questions if he went prowling around during the night.'

She took longer over that one, frowning at the view beyond the glass. 'I'd certainly like to think Eleanor wasn't involved. She – well, it's an old-fashioned word but she's too nice. But I'll go along with the rest of it.'

'Good.' The irony of the whole position made Carrick wonder. If Robertson hadn't been so willing to make a fool of his wife in front of guests, if his wife hadn't found that package of photographs waiting in the mail ... out of insignificance they'd become pointers which led to so much of the rest.

Mora stirred uneasily. 'But how does Peter Leslie come into it?'

'He almost certainly didn't at the beginning,' said Carrick grimly. 'My guess is he kept quiet about the *Clavella*'s real reason for coming here. Though it must have been a strain once he found out more about Eleanor Robertson. She has the kind of friends who could make real trouble from what he had to offer.'

'You make them sound like headcases,' protested Mora. 'There's nothing wrong with having ideals.'

'I didn't say there was,' murmured Carrick. 'Given the chance, I might have a few myself. Want to hear the rest?'

She nodded and stayed quiet.

'Suppose Robertson played along with Leslie because he wanted to keep as many tabs as he could on the *Clavella*. Then when Leslie decided to make his break wouldn't he try to contact the nearest people who might help him? Once he got clear of the harbour Robertson's garage is fairly near, a lot nearer than the house.'

'That phone call from the garage?' asked Mora quietly.

'From the foreman.' Carrick nodded. 'The timing fits.'

Neither of them spoke for a moment. Outside, the wind seemed to have dropped again. But a few hints of dark cloud were beginning to appear on the horizon.

Mora spoke first. 'Suppose Robertson does have him?'

'Then he'll want to move Leslie out of here as soon as he can. Probably by sea, because that's his best chance – or it will be, if he can do it before the weather breaks completely. Once that happens his chance has gone.'

Nodding thoughtfully she stubbed her cigarette in the dashboard ashtray. 'He'll try for tonight?'

'I would.' He wished there was a way around the next part. 'Where's Robertson right now?'

'He went to the garage but he'll be home for lunch. Why?'

'Andy couldn't find a radio at the garage, maybe because Robertson has it at home. We need someone to search that house, Mora.' He paused, seeing by her face that she understood. 'Someone who could do it without any fuss or suspicion.'

'Meaning me.' She took it calmly. 'Looking for a radio's one thing. Suppose I opened a cupboard and Peter Leslie popped out?'

'Robertson wouldn't run that kind of risk. I'm willing to bet Eleanor Robertson doesn't even guess what's going on.'

'With me as side-stake?' She grimaced but nodded. 'All right, I'll do it.'

'Be careful,' emphasized Carrick. 'I mean that – I don't want you running any risks. We can always try another way. You're – well, I don't want anything happening to you.'

'It won't.' She gave him a small, half-appraising, half-encouraging smile. 'Webb, I never did pretend I'd been close to Andy.'

'I know.'

125

He put a gentle but purposeful arm round her shoulders and she came willingly, lips meeting his, the warm scent of her body suddenly in his nostrils. They kissed again, her mouth more demanding now, a soft sound coming low in her throat as his other hand moved gently beneath the anorak to cup over her breast. Then she drew back a little, squirming round until her head rested on his shoulder.

'I'll tell you one thing,' she murmured.

'What?' Carrick nibbled her ear.

'If this happens again we'll use my car.' Her eyes twinkled. 'It's a damned sight more comfortable. Either I move soon or this gear lever is going to cause me an alarming injury.'

She eased away, produced a lipstick and comb, used them, then nodded. 'Ready. You can drop me off at the road end on the way. What about afterwards?'

'Come into Quinbegg. But don't rush – leave it till the afternoon so that there's no fuss. Contact me or Commander Dobie.'

Mora nodded calmly. 'And if anything does go wrong?'

'It shouldn't. I'll stop at Robertson's garage when I get back and keep him there as long as I can.' He leaned over, kissed her again, then started the engine.

Harvey Robertson was in his showroom, making a sales pitch to a customer across the front of a late-model Austin 1300. The car was a bright yellow job, the customer a suspicious-eyed hill farmer in baggy suit and heavy boots. Coming in quietly, Carrick strolled past them and pretended to inspect a rack of car accessories while the discussion went on.

Suddenly the farmer gave a willing nod of agreement and held out his hand to seal the bargain.

126

Robertson gripped it then smiled as he escorted the man to the door.

'She'll be ready after lunch,' he said cheerfully. 'But I'll tell you this – I'm not making much money on this deal.' The smile stayed in place until he'd closed the door again then twisted cynically at the edges as he turned to Carrick.

'Today's battle – they'd argue for an hour if it saved a penny.'

'He fought you down?' queried Carrick.

'By fifty quid – he thinks.' Robertson winked. 'I'd have come down seventy-five. Give me a minute till I get hold of Kip. I promised we'd fit new seat belts.' He crossed over, used the showroom telephone, then came back. 'Found Leslie yet?'

Carrick shook his head.

'You're having your share of troubles.' Robertson's fleshy face crinkled in sympathetic concern. 'What's it all about anyway? The stories going around are pretty wild and when I saw Sergeant MacKenzie this morning he just made noises.'

'The submersible business. It wasn't an accident.'

'And Leslie –' The man's thick lips shaped a whistle.

'It fits.' Carrick leaned against the Austin's door. 'And it involves you, incidentally.'

'Meaning what?' Robertson's expression didn't alter. Except for the eyes – for a fractional moment they flickered warily.

'You had a break-in here. It happened a couple of nights before Captain Jeffrey and Humbey were killed.'

'That's right.' Robertson waited stolidly.

'Sergeant MacKenzie thought it might have been kids. But they didn't take anything.' Carrick raised an eyebrow. 'Or – well, did they?'

'Nothing that mattered.' Robertson scratched a

hand along his chin. 'Maybe a few hand tools, but we can't be sure.'

'And maybe a length of copper piping, a short length?'

'That's possible,' conceded Robertson, frowning. 'Hell, I don't keep inventory on every bit of metal lying around.' He stopped, as if suddenly understanding. 'Hand tools, piping – wait a minute. Are you saying –'

'We've got most things on the *Clavella* but there are usually people around, people who might remember later, particularly if someone had been trying to rig a homemade bomb.'

'Leslie?' It had to be an act. But Carrick's conviction came close to wavering at the shocked surprise the man injected into his voice. 'I can't believe it. We – heck, we had him out at the house a few times. Eleanor found him interesting and I got along with him. He looked the quiet type.'

'That's still how we figure it.' The first lie was always the hardest, decided Carrick. 'We recovered some fragments of the bomb, including a section of copper piping which certainly wasn't *Clavella* stock.'

Robertson frowned gravely. 'How can I help?'

'By letting me look around here, starting with where he got in.'

Robertson nodded and led the way.

The break-in had been a crude win-or-lose affair with access through a rear window after breaking the glass. From there they moved on, Carrick stretching the inspection tour to the limit, knowing from Robertson's willingness that he was wasting time – yet having that same time-wasting as his main objective. He made it last for almost an hour, from stores area to toilet block, conscious of the interest directed his way by Robertson's foreman and the two mechanics.

128

There was plenty of copper piping lying around. He had one of the mechanics cut a few small samples then turned apologetically to Robertson.

'Sorry, but we don't want to miss any possibilities.'

'You haven't,' said Robertson with a weary, fraying patience. 'Finished?' He took Carrick's nod with open relief and glanced at his watch. 'Time I was heading home. But I've got to be back this afternoon to settle that car sale.' Coming closer, he lowered his voice. 'Look, how dangerous is Leslie?'

Carrick carefully matched his manner. 'He has a gun and he used it – even if he didn't manage to hit anyone. For the rest, I don't know. We're dealing with what may be a complete mental breakdown.'

'Little green men again?' Robertson grimaced. 'What worries me is he could head for our place. Even with Mora there I'm not happy about Eleanor being more or less on her own. I think I'll send Kip out for the afternoon – he could give my boat engine a service while he's there. No sense in him just hanging around.'

Whatever else Harvey Robertson might or might not be, decided Carrick, he certainly didn't miss a move.

Quinbegg police station and Sergeant MacKenzie bore a strong resemblance to twin victims of a successful take-over bid. A chart of the North Minch had been pinned over the charge-room noticeboard. In shirt sleeves, two of the *Clavella*'s ratings in close attendance, Commander Dobie showed every sign of considering permanent residence. As Carrick entered, the telephone rang. It was answered by the nearest rating, leaving Sergeant MacKenzie unhappily in the background.

'Back already?' Dobie greeted him cheerfully enough, which was a reasonable start. 'Well, we've made some progress. How about you?'

'Some – at least I think so, sir,' reported Carrick crisply.

'Good.' Dobie stopped as the rating replaced the telephone receiver. The man shook his head. 'Well, you can hear my side first, Carrick. The most important item is your Russian trawler. She's been spotted.'

'Where, sir?' Carrick followed him eagerly towards the chart.

'Here.' Dobie tapped a small, energetic forefinger at a spot on the far side of the North Minch. 'She's anchored in a bay south of Cellar Head.'

It was a long way from the mainland, further than he'd expected, yet ideal for a vessel seeking either shelter or privacy. Cellar Head, on the east coast of the long island of Lewis, was a virtually uninhabited section of gravel bays separated by rocky points and fringed by low cliffs. Fishing was poor to non-existent, visitors few.

'*Skua* made the identification,' said Dobie happily. 'She's Russian all right, their XA 417 – a regular in the Minch.' His finger traced busily. 'I've ordered *Skua* to continue north then lie in here at Braga Rock, acting as a radar picket. And right now *Marlin* is doing the same thing on our side of the Minch, south of Handa Island. Whichever way that trawler moves we've got her bottled.'

'Which helps,' agreed Carrick thankfully. He looked around. 'Where's Clapper, sir?'

'Doing a little job for me.' Dobie gave the kind of smile which discouraged further questioning. 'You'll hear about it later, if I'm right. He's out with Preacher again – that skippers' meeting didn't last long and ended in another deadlock.' Deliberately he glanced at MacKenzie. 'Sergeant, what else have we got?'

'The post mortem reports, sir.' The policeman seemed woefully glad that his existence had been remembered.

'Which are pretty much what we expected,' said Dobie shortly. 'Humbey killed outright, Andy Jeffrey drowned. There's a preliminary report on the submersible – again nothing we didn't know or guess. It was plastic explosive and a pressure fuse.' His voice gained an ice-flecked edge. 'And by the experts' reckoning whoever put it together did a highly professional job.'

Carrick nodded absently, the details incidental. 'Leslie?'

Sergeant MacKenzie chuckled from the background. 'Nothing apart from a false alarm. The army found a character halfway up a mountain on the An Socach ridge, about twelve miles inland, an' dragged him down. The poor devil wasn't very pleased. He'd been trying to climb the thing for the best part of a week.'

'Hardly hilarious,' said Dobie severely but with a twinkle in his eyes. 'All right, Carrick – your turn.'

Carrick told him, conscious of MacKenzie's gathering frown. When he finished, Dobie's expression was pretty much the same.

'Robertson – he called in here this morning, offering to help.' Dobie stood where he was, eyes closed, thinking aloud. 'You haven't really much to go on. Not enough to hang a budgie. Still, the way things are –'

He crossed to the telephone, stopped, shook his head, and sighed. 'Sorry, sergeant, but I won't trust the telephone service with this one. We'll radio it from the *Clavella*, coded. I want a full security vetting on husband and wife. Carrick, when do you expect the Atholl girl to make contact with us?'

'The earliest she can, but I told her to play it naturally – that could mean any time this afternoon.'

'She'd have to eat with them, I suppose,' agreed Dobie with a touch of irritation.

'That's probably the least of her worries.'

'I know.' Dobie made something close to an apologetic noise. 'Waiting never was one of my strong points. Anyway, I was going to suggest we might as well eat too.'

'I can fix tea and sandwiches,' volunteered Sergeant MacKenzie.

A faint shudder ran through Commander Dobie's small figure. 'You can, sergeant. For yourself . . . I presume you won't want to abandon your post. I'll be on the *Clavella*. We'll – ah – find something there.'

Slipping on his jacket, he beckoned Carrick to the door. They were outside and on their way to the harbour before he spoke again.

'Bell told me about Preacher's gift.' He smiled happily. 'I suggested lobster thermidor to the galley, and I happen to know you have an excellent unopened –' he glanced at Carrick and saw no contradiction – 'so far unopened bottle of whisky in your cabin.'

Carrick nodded ruefully. 'It beats sandwiches and tea.'

'Agreed.' Dobie quickened his pace a little as the harbour appeared ahead. 'Never do battle on an empty stomach, laddie. I make it a golden rule.' He nodded politely to a passing fisherman. 'Yes, a golden rule. Have you thought of the real problem in all this, Carrick?'

'Sir?'

'We're talking in terms of a trawler pick-up. But suppose there's a Soviet nuclear submarine out there still – suppose she gets the job?' He strode on, whistling between his teeth for a moment. 'Yes, one

132

wrong move and either of us could end up being the man who started World War Three. Quite a notion, eh?'

Carrick swallowed. And fixed his mind on that waiting bottle.

Chapter Seven

On the turn again, the tide was coming in fast – but in a very different way from usual. A rippling, oily swell replaced the previous wavelets, a swell which lapped the harbour wall with barely a splash. Dark clouds hung heavy to the west, the wind had paused for breath and the very air felt chill and listless. Along the quayside most boats had extra lines ashore and additional car-tyre fenders in position.

The storm was on its way. Hours might pass before the full fury arrived. But the white seabirds winging inland told the same story as the black warning cones being hoisted on the signal mast at the harbour entrance. A Force Ten forecast . . . a whole gale, wind velocities of sixty miles an hour, one stage short of a full hurricane. In the days of the old sailing clippers a ship's master would have muttered a prayer then called for close-reefed running. His modern counterpart still treated Force Ten with equal fear and preparation.

But Commander Dobie had shut such matters – and most others – from his mind. From the moment he and Carrick entered the privacy of the *Clavella*'s tiny wardroom his whole attitude underwent a change as if one set of switches had been closed and another opened.

Arriving on schedule, the lobster thermidor met his qualified approval. Which, decided Carrick, was probably more of a compliment to the single-malt whisky beside it. The *Clavella's* galley had done their best. But he'd have wagered the cook-steward probably imagined *cordon bleu* had something to do with a French football team.

Dobie talked as he ate, mentioning fragments of Department gossip at just high enough a level to have normally held Carrick's interest. Yet Carrick found his mind wandering, tried not to fidget, and it came as a sudden surprise to realize his guest had changed back to practicalities.

'I said the navy are mounting a full radio monitoring watch,' repeated Dobie, forking another mouthful of pink lobster flesh. 'They haven't reported anything so far and they'd miss any signals sent last night.' He chewed for a moment. 'You know, this isn't really too bad. I think –' He broke off, an eyebrow rising as the wardroom door swung open and Sam Paxton panted in.

'Sir –'

'Junior officers should knock,' said Dobie coldly. 'What is it?'

The mate swallowed, flushed, then blurted on, 'There's a body floating into the harbour. It looks like Peter Leslie, sir.'

'Really?' Dobie took the news with a disciplined calm and frowned a little as Carrick half-rose from his chair. 'Well, Mr Paxton, I'm certainly not jumping in to find out. Bring it aboard. Two men, a dinghy and a boathook – go along with them. We'll be on deck shortly.'

'Aye aye, sir.' Scarlet, beard twitching with embarrassment, Paxton gave a quick salute and scrambled off.

'Don't look so damned irate, Carrick,' murmured Dobie. He carefully topped up his glass from the single-malt bottle and smiled wryly. 'I didn't expect it this way either. But did you really imagine we'd a chance of getting Leslie back in a walking, talking state?'

'I hadn't thought that far ahead,' said Carrick woodenly.

'I had. But I'm a professional pessimist.' Dobie drained the full glass and eased back his chair with a sigh. 'Well, I suppose we'd better go before you burst. With any luck Leslie may still have some answers for us.'

They went on deck. The m.f.v.'s dinghy was already in the water, the rest of the *Clavella*'s crew were lining the port rail and a growing audience were watching along the quayside.

Floating face down, rolling a little as each oily swell washed it further into the harbour, the corpse was still a full fifty yards off. But there was no mistaking the quilted blue kapok jacket and sodden grey slacks.

'Leslie?' asked Dobie.

Carrick nodded, beckoned a deckhand, and thumbed towards the village. 'Tell Sergeant MacKenzie.'

The man went off. Out on the water, the dinghy went about its sombre task. Using the boathook from the stern, Sam Paxton brought the body wallowing nearer, gripped it by the collar, then signalled the men at the oars. They began pulling again. Leslie's body in tow, the dinghy returned to the quay, came alongside a flight of stone steps, and was steadied there by a fisherman. Another *Clavella* rating was already waiting with a folded stretcher.

Minutes later the aft deckhouse was again in use as a temporary mortuary. Hands clasped behind his back, face an expressionless mask, Dobie stood for a moment watching the water drip from the dead man's clothing.

'Mostly the jacket that kept him afloat,' he murmured to himself. He paused and glanced at Paxton. 'Secure the dinghy, laddie. Then keep people out of here.'

Thankfully, the mate departed.

'Sir?' Carrick gestured towards Leslie. Dobie nodded, and he carefully unzipped the jacket. It had a deep inner pocket, button fastened. More water kept up its monotonous dripping to the deck as Carrick opened the pocket, felt inside, and drew out a large, fat, sodden envelope.

'I'll do it.' Dobie took the envelope, opened it, and carefully examined the sheets of folded paper which had been within. 'Humbey's notes all right. Film?'

Quietly, hating the job, Carrick checked the rest of the dead man's pockets and shook his head.

'Any marks of violence?'

'None I can see, sir.'

'That's a medical man's job anyway.' Dobie sighed, turned away, and held one of the sheets of paper up against the sunlight coming through a porthole. After a moment he did the same with the others. 'Carrick –'

'Sir?' Carrick came over.

'Look at the corners on this one. See the pinprick holes?' As Carrick nodded Dobie's mouth tightened. 'If you had some folded sheets of paper and wanted to make a good, fast photocopy job you know what you'd do? Pin 'em to a board. If you were careless – or pushed for time at any rate.' He hummed softly to himself for a moment. 'We all make mistakes, eh?'

Carrick stared at him. 'You mean he's a deliberate plant?'

'That's a crude verdict on a fairly clever piece of thinking,' protested Dobie mildly. 'We're looking for Leslie and the whole area is screwed down tight, too tight for some people's comfort. So they give us Leslie plus the papers –'

'But not the film, sir.'

Dobie sighed. 'Man, if it hadn't been that Preacher couldn't resist nosing through what Leslie left with him we'd never have known the film existed.'

Slowly, Carrick nodded. 'Undeveloped film – so even Leslie didn't know what was on it.'

'Exactly.' Dobie picked up a folded blanket and carefully draped it over the dead man's body, covering the face. 'He didn't know but they'd want to find out. We can make a darned good guess that it concerns submarine activity in the Trench. But remember, the opposition are probably still hoping our whole panic is over losing the seafire papers, that we don't realize anything else was taken.'

'So they send us back the papers, special delivery, to make us happy,' said Carrick bitterly.

'Correct,' agreed Dobie blandly. 'Which means we're dealing with someone who knows his local tides and currents, knows them well enough to be sure that if Leslie was launched at a certain time and place he'd turn up somewhere near the harbour . . . and quickly, with that kapok jacket to keep him reasonably afloat.'

Callously, cleverly done. Carrick wondered how long Leslie had been kept alive and exactly how he had died. Even the autopsy report might find it difficult to provide the answers. It was never easy to estimate time of death when a body was recovered from the sea. There were too many outside factors, from water temperature onwards. Cause of death? It was fairly easy to tap a man on the head then hold him under water, hard to prove it had happened that way. Though if you wanted to pretend a man had drowned at sea you certainly didn't dump him in the bath and turn the taps on. It had to be salt water, which would correctly increase the chloride content of the blood some forty per cent by its action through the lungs and heart.

He remembered a cherub-faced pathologist who'd thumped that one home at basic training lectures, part of a happy little half-hour talk on drowning at sea. Nobody had felt much like lunch when the man had finished.

'Carrick –' Dobie's murmur and the sound of a familiar voice outside brought him back to the present. 'Enter Sergeant MacKenzie. I'll deal with him. I suggest you go ashore and telephone the Robertsons. If you happen to be right about them, a few relieved noises might pay dividends.'

Sergeant MacKenzie came into the deckhouse as Carrick left. From the look on the county man's face Commander Dobie was going to have an interesting time.

There was a telephone box near the harbour gates. Dialling Harvey Robertson's home number, he had to wait only a few seconds before the ringing tone ended on a sudden click. Robertson's voice answered and the garage owner greeted him with a detached, almost guarded formality.

'If you've more questions about the break-in –'

'No,' Carrick assured him. 'That can wait now. But I knew you were worried about leaving your wife alone. That's over – we found Leslie.'

'Good.' It came with a breath of relief. Which might have been for more than one reason. 'How?'

'Dead, floating in the harbour,' said Carrick shortly. 'Drowned – the tide brought him in.'

'I see.' The line was silent for a moment. 'Suicide, eh?'

'That's how it looks,' said Carrick deliberately.

'Well, I appreciate being told,' said Robertson. 'I'll let Eleanor know straight away, and Mora. We can certainly stop worrying now.'

'Is Mora around?' Nursing the receiver against his shoulder, Carrick glanced at his watch. It was a little after two thirty, early for her to have left for Quinbegg. But there was no harm in finding out.

'Yes, in the kitchen helping Eleanor wash up – we've just finished lunch,' replied Robertson easily. 'Hold on and I'll get her.'

A couple of minutes passed then Mora's voice came on the line.

'I've heard, Webb,' she said quietly. 'That's why you were kept waiting.'

'Leslie?' He guessed that she wasn't alone. 'Well, it's nasty but it certainly eases the pressure at this end.'

'Yes.' It came slowly, uncertainly. 'Does it mean you'll be busy this afternoon? I mean – well, we can forget that arrangement if you want. I've no real reason for coming.'

Carrick mentally awarded her top marks for the way she was handling the opportunity. For the benefit of any listener, he played along. 'I'd still like to see you, unless it creates any problems.'

'No,' she assured quickly. 'Everything's fine with me. But there's no sense in my coming unless . . .' Her voice died away awkwardly.

'Let's keep the date as it stands,' he suggested. 'Come in when you can. Right?'

'Fine,' she said, and sounded cheerful again.

He hung up, left the telephone box, and stood for a moment. Mora had spelled it out clearly enough. She'd looked and she'd found nothing. Maybe his hunch was wrong, maybe he'd been wasting time. He sighed, gave up, and headed back to the *Clavella*.

* * *

The m.f.v.'s little chartroom was a busy place when he reached it. Commander Dobie and Sam Paxton were in occupancy, Dobie frowning over an unrolled chart of the North Minch, the mate hovering attentively at his shoulder.

'Did you speak to Robertson?' Dobie didn't bother to look up.

'Yes, and to Mora.' Carrick watched as Dobie made a quick measurement with dividers and a rule. 'She drew a blank – that's what she seemed to be trying to say.'

'I'm not surprised,' said Dobie peevishly, flicking a radio room signal form across the chartroom table. 'This came in soon after you left. The navy's monitoring units have picked up a high-speed Morse transmission coming from the mainland – and the Soviet trawler over at Cellar Head has been answering. As near as our people can calculate the shore signals originated from an area about fifteen miles south of here.'

Carrick winced. 'Are they positive, sir?'

'Not pin-point sure,' snapped Dobie. 'The shore transmission didn't last long enough for exact cross-bearings. But they've a firm general location, which means we've something definite to work on.' He grunted under his breath. 'Forget about Robertson for now. All we had there were a few coincidences and they damned nearly led us in the wrong direction.'

Glumly, Carrick nodded. It certainly looked that way.

'No sudden bright ideas this time, mister?' asked Dobie sardonically.

'None in sight, sir,' he admitted.

'Right now that's no cause for grief as far as I'm concerned.' Dobie scowled again at the chart. 'And add this to the collection. According to Sergeant Mac-Kenzie the most likely spot to launch Leslie's body and have it washed in here would be to the south.'

141

'He was pretty sure of that,' volunteered Paxton, then fell silent under Dobie's glare.

'I'll take his word,' said Carrick woodenly. 'How did he feel about the rest of it?'

Dobie gave a dry, humourless laugh. 'Nothing will ever surprise Sergeant MacKenzie again. But he'll play it our way, get Leslie's body removed ashore – more business for your friend Robertson's ambulance – and spread the word that it looks like suicide. I've a feeling that'll get to the right ears fairly quickly.'

'And after that, sir?' asked Carrick, looking at the area Dobie had circled on the chart. It was a rocky, deserted-looking stretch of coastline with probably half a hundred places where a small boat could come in to pick up a man.

'After that we make a real production of everything being happy again.' Dobie's manner changed, became almost sympathetic. 'For a start, you'll give shore leave to all hands except for your usual harbour watch and the radio operator. Tell them there's no need to be back aboard before midnight.'

'But –' Carrick almost choked on his surprise – 'but that'll mean we're completely out of action.'

'Yes.'

'And what happens when the trawler moves?' demanded Carrick stubbornly.

'What happens?' Dobie treated him patiently. 'Sorry, but you're that old cliché a small cog in a big wheel. I've got two fishery cruisers in position, each with three times the speed and size of the *Clavella*. They'll handle the trawler, the police will take care of the shore end, and I'll be leaving to be down there as soon as the situation starts to shape. Your part is finished.'

'Yes, sir.' Wearily, Carrick nodded to Paxton. 'Hands to shore leave, Sam. I'll be around.'

* * *

142

Robertson's ambulance didn't appear on the quayside until four o'clock. By then the m.f.v.'s hull was rocking gently in the increased harbour swell. The wind had gradually returned and the low clouds stretched across the horizon were drawing perceptibly nearer.

The driver was one of Robertson's mechanics in a dark raincoat and peaked hat. Opening the vehicle's rear doors he waited for two of the *Clavella*'s deckhands to help him carry a plain basket shell aboard. They made a slower return journey within a matter of minutes, loaded Leslie's body into the ambulance, and it drove off.

Half an hour later the first of the clouds arrived overhead and what began as a light drizzle quickly became a heavy downpour. But it soon ended – and as the sun broke through again Preacher Noah's boat came pitching in through the heavy swell at the harbour entrance.

Alone on deck, most of the m.f.v.'s crew long since ashore, Carrick watched the scarred old lifeboat throttle back in the calmer water then come alongside under little more than steerage way. Grinning up at him from the helm, using a deft combination of rudder and throttle to hold his boat against the *Clavella*'s hull, Preacher waited while his passengers scrambled up and over.

Allison left first, took a couple of heavy wooden boxes passed up to him by Haydock, then waited till his friend joined him. Taking a box each, they vanished in the direction of the research area. Clapper Bell crossed last, giving Preacher's thin back a friendly slap as he left. The boat's engine barked, Preacher spun the wheel, and the battered craft swung away in a foul-smelling cloud of blue exhaust smoke.

Giving a farewell wave, Bell turned from the rail and strolled over to join Carrick.

143

'Reportin' back, sir,' he said with a mock formality then winked cheerfully. 'An' damned glad too. That sea's getting pretty lumpy, believe me.'

'It'll get worse,' said Carrick shortly. 'What were those two boy wonders doing?'

'Meaning you don't know either?' Bell rubbed a puzzled hand along his chin. 'I asked, but they gave me the kind o' grin which says "You're an ignorant slob, Clapper," so I didn't push it. All we did was go out to the Quinbegg Trench, lower some wee bottles over the side an' fill them wi' sea water.'

'Nothing else?'

'Nothing.' Bell frowned around. 'Where's everyone hidin', sir?'

'Gone ashore, spreading gladness.' Carrick shrugged and in a few short sentences told him what had happened.

'We do the work but we don't get to see the excitement, eh?' The bo'sun's crumpled face darkened and his voice boomed angrily. 'That's typical of the shrivelled wee bastard!'

'Shut up,' warned Carrick softly. 'He's coming now.'

Emerging from the wheelhouse, Dobie clambered down and approached them with an odd glint in his eyes. But if he'd heard he gave no hint.

'Any sign of that girl yet?' he asked brusquely.

Carrick shook his head.

'Well, she's safe enough.' Dobie clasped his hands behind his back and let himself sway with the deck's roll. 'I've had a signal about the Robertsons – hardly worth the trouble of decoding. Security know the woman as a bash-a-copper type demonstrator at peace rallies. But they've nothing, absolutely nothing on her husband. Satisfied?'

The sun faded as another dark cloud slid overhead. A few splashes of rain darkened the deck at their feet.

Frowning at Carrick's lack of response, Dobie cleared his throat in icy fashion.

'Anyway, that's incidental. I'm leaving – the navy monitor stations have picked up another Morse transmission from the same location down south and pretty well pin-pointed it this time. I'll let you know what happens, don't worry. You've – ah – done a damned good job, both of you.'

'Thanks,' said Carrick neutrally. He considered the Chief Superintendent of Fisheries, hearing the rising wind beginning to draw a thin, quavering note from their antenna wires. 'Sir, what do you want these water samples for?'

'Research.' Dobie unbent a little. 'An idea I have about that seafire bloom. But –' he shook his head – 'no, I'm not going out on a limb about it yet.'

Bell grunted with a near insolence.

'You said something?' asked Dobie menacingly.

Sam Paxton saved the day, scurrying towards them from the radio room. He had a message form in his hand and Dobie needed only one glance.

'That's it,' he said softly, Clapper Bell forgotten. 'The trawler is on the move. According to *Skua* she's clearing Cellar Head and steering south-west. The rendezvous is on.' He glanced at his watch, sucking on his lips. 'Say two hours till sunset – and our Soviet friend will need four hours, maybe more, to get across if this storm keeps building.' His hands rubbed together. 'Which gives us plenty of time to be organized, eh?'

Ten minutes later Dobie had gone, collected from the harbour by an anonymous grey car which already held three sombre-faced Naval Security men in civilian clothes. Watching it go, Carrick's feelings were mixed. Maybe Dobie was right and the whole scene had shifted from Quinbegg. But Mora still hadn't arrived and it hadn't been Dobie who'd asked her to go back to the Robertsons' house.

A sudden, heavier downpour of rain pattered along the deck. Swearing mildly, Clapper Bell turned up the collar of his monkey-jacket.

'How about me buyin' you a drink, sir?' he said hopefully. He sighed at Carrick's headshake. 'Still thinkin' about that girl? You could always call her again and –'

Reluctantly, Carrick shook his head. 'Not yet, Clapper. But do me a favour and stay here for a spell in case she shows up. I'm going to see Sergeant MacKenzie.'

'And after that?' demanded Bell suspiciously.

'I wish I knew,' admitted Carrick.

The rain was steadily worsening. Collecting an oil-skin coat from the wheelhouse, he pulled it on and went ashore. As he walked along the quayside a swell heavier than the rest broke like thunder against the outer breakwater and sent a curtain of spray high and white into the air. The Force Ten approaching was flexing its muscles.

Sergeant MacKenzie wasn't exactly the portrait of an energetic guardian of the law. Tunic unbuttoned, tie loosened, he had a collection of small tins arranged along the police office counter and worked over them with a surprisingly nimble-fingered concentration. Flickering a glance as Carrick entered he grunted a welcome and carefully fed a tiny red feather into the minute pattern of others he'd assembled. Two fast twists of tough nylon thread lashed the feather in place, completing the tailing over a viciously barbed salmon hook. He bit the nylon off short with his teeth, beamed in satisfaction, and turned his full attention to his visitor.

'Just passing the time now the panic's died down,' he said in partial apology. 'I do a bit o' river fishing when I get the chance. Always prefer my own flies.' A gentle forefinger stroked his latest creation. 'This is the kind I call "Barbara's Butcher" after my wife.'

'Very nice.' Carrick waited patiently as the tins were swept out of sight.

'Now then –' MacKenzie closed a drawer and frowned at the rain still dripping from Carrick's oilskin – 'take that off if you're staying, man. I'd say you and me are in the same boat, so to speak. Nobody wants us any more.'

'What do you make of it all?' asked Carrick, taking him at his word and hanging the oilskin on a peg.

MacKenzie pursed his lips whimsically. 'Och, I'm a country cop, not particularly paid to think. I've had a hard job just keeping up with things.'

'Including Leslie floating in.'

'Aye. Robertson's ambulance is taking him to Inverness straight off. It suits them to do it now and there's no sense in having a body lying around here needless like when the post mortem will be at Inverness anyway.' MacKenzie took the cigarette Carrick offered and accepted a light. 'Sorry about the delay before I could get them to collect but that's the only ambulance around here and it seems they had another job in the next parish.'

'Maybe we should have made an advance booking,' said Carrick dryly.

The policeman grinned a little and let some smoke drift happily from his nostrils. 'Anyway, chief officer, the excitement's over as far as Quinbegg's concerned. That's for sure.'

'Is it?' Carrick eyed thoughtfully. 'Suppose I said I still wasn't happy about things here?'

147

MacKenzie blinked. 'Why, man? If it's the Robertsons, the commander said the Atholl girl –'

'Hasn't arrived yet,' said Carrick, cutting him short.

'Och, maybe her car broke down,' suggested
MacKenzie, relaxing again. 'Give the Robertsons a
phone from here if you're worried about her.'

Carrick shook his head. 'I want to hear from you
first. You've had time to think about the Robertsons.'

MacKenzie nodded.

'Well?'

'There's a thing or two I wondered about,' admitted
MacKenzie slowly. 'That garage, for instance. The girl
on the pumps is local but the foreman an' his two
mechanics are outsiders, men he hired after he bought
the place.' He hesitated. 'Then – well, let's just say I've
never known how Robertson made any money out o'
the business! The last man had only one mechanic and
still went bust.'

'Nothing else?'

MacKenzie grinned. 'Well, I'm just no' very fond of
the man.'

Carrick drew a deep breath. 'I think I'll use that
phone now, sergeant.'

The Robertsons' home number rang for what
seemed a long time before it was answered, this time
by Eleanor Robertson.

'You, Mr Carrick!' She sounded bright and yet
slightly nervous. 'That's a stroke of luck. I was just
wondering how to contact you!'

Sergeant MacKenzie at his side and straining to
hear both ends of the conversation, Carrick chose his
words carefully. 'I thought I'd check on whether Mora
had left yet – she's coming in to meet me but I could
be delayed.'

'She's here but –' Eleanor Robertson's voice hesitated – 'well, I'm afraid she won't be leaving. In fact

she's lying down, Mr Carrick. She isn't feeling too well.'

'What's wrong?' Carrick tried to keep his tone level and his concern mild.

'Nothing serious,' assured Eleanor Robertson quickly. 'She suddenly just felt very tired and more than a little shaky. It's probably reaction to all that's been going on. But she needs rest, and after that she should be fine again.'

'I could come out.'

'No – no, I wouldn't do that,' declared the woman. 'She's sleeping now. I'll look after her, Mr Carrick. I've no medals for nursing, of course.' A sound like a nervous giggle of emphasis came over the line. 'In fact, no medals at all – but we'll manage.'

The line went dead.

MacKenzie shrugged and waited till Carrick replaced the receiver. 'There's your explanation.'

'Is it?' Carrick's face was grim. What he'd heard was logical and reasonable. Except for one thing. Twice Eleanor Robertson had said 'no medals', twice he'd felt a stab of memory at how he'd used that self-same phrase to Mora, with a very different significance. If Mora had remembered, if for some strange reason Eleanor Robertson had been trying to pass a message to him . . .

There was only one way to find out. Shrugging back into the oilskin coat he answered MacKenzie's unspoken curiosity.

'I'm going out there, social call style.'

Frowning, MacKenzie automatically began fastening his tunic. 'Well, if you want me along –'

'No.' He shook his head firmly. 'Stay and tie yourself another couple of salmon flies, sergeant. Give me an hour then if I haven't contacted you get hold of Paxton or Clapper Bell. But whatever you do after that go gently . . . and carefully.'

'You sound like my wife,' said MacKenzie wryly. 'But if that's how you want it, fair enough. I'll be hoping you're wrong.'

The rain had eased a little but the sky was a heavy grey blanket of cloud and the wind strong enough to rock the Department station wagon on its springs. Carrick took the north road from the village, driving with a cold concentration, wasting no time. He passed Robertson's garage, noticed it appeared to be closed for the night, and gripped the wheel tighter as another gust shook the station wagon. Twigs, leaves and other debris whipped across the tarmac ahead, swept along by the same westerly blast.

Should he have tried to contact Dobie before he left? He shrugged, doubting if the Chief Superintendent of Fisheries would have thanked him. What could he have reported anyway? That he was going to check on why a girl hadn't kept a date? Yes, Dobie would have loved being interrupted in his planning to be advised of that gem of information.

The road was almost deserted at that hour. A couple of farm trucks heading in towards Quinbegg constituted the only traffic he encountered and in a very short time the road-end track to Robertson's house appeared ahead. Carrick slowed the station wagon, let it bounce down the rutted track towards the shore at a sedate pace, then dropped down another gear as the house came into view.

Two cars, Mora's MG and a neat Jaguar coupé, were already lying in the parking area. The station wagon rolled to a halt beside them, he switched off, climbed out, and quickly pulled his hat lower on his head as the wind tried to snatch it. The pulsing thunder of breaking seas was loud in his ears and he glanced towards the water – then stiffened.

Robertson's sailing boat was lying a few yards off shore, swinging and tugging at her moorings in the light but broken swell which penetrated past the sheltering barrier of the hog-back rock. He eyed it again as he began crunching across the gravel towards the front door of the house. Its mast had been stepped, and a powerful outboard motor was mounted on the stern transom.

The *Anna* was ready to sail. But where? Few sane men would contemplate taking any kind of small craft out into the weather that lay waiting. Not unless they had fairly desperate reasons.

Reaching the door, he pressed the bell-push and waited. It opened, Eleanor Robertson looked out, and in that single moment he knew he'd been right. There was a nervous fear on her round face as she tried to smile.

'Mr Carrick – you'd better come in!'

He did, she closed the door against the wind, and he glanced around. They seemed alone in the hallway, the whole house silent and brooding.

'I was worried about Mora,' he said loudly. 'I thought I'd better come out and see how she was.'

Staring at him, Eleanor Robertson moistened her lips. 'Still asleep – just like I told you. I think – well, she's best left alone.'

'I won't wake her,' he promised. 'But suppose you let me see her, Mrs Robertson? She's a fairly special responsibility as far as I'm concerned.'

'No.' The woman took a step nearer and suddenly he realized that she was trying hard to convey a warning with her eyes. 'I think you should go, Mr Carrick. I –' one hand rubbed anxiously against her side – 'yes, please go now.'

Deliberately, he made his choice. 'I'm not leaving till I've seen her, Mrs Robertson.'

Her shoulders slumped and her mouth quivered. 'Please –'

'Sorry.' Carrick moved to go past her.

Then stopped. A door had swung open a few feet away. Harvey Robertson stood framed in the opening, an automatic pistol held steadily in one hand, the muzzle pointing squarely at Carrick's stomach.

'Stay very still,' said Robertson almost sadly. As he came nearer his wife moved back against the wall. 'Kip –'

Grinning, the thick-set foreman emerged from the same room, a machine-pistol cradled at his hip.

'Having a party?' queried Carrick mildly.

Robertson grunted to himself. 'Eleanor, go back to the lounge and stay there.' As she went off, white-faced, he considered Carrick again. 'Well, I didn't want it this way. But that woman put on such a damned awful act –' He stopped and nodded to his companion. 'Check him, Kip.'

Spun round to face the wall, forced to clasp his hands behind his neck, Carrick was quickly and expertly frisked. Finished, Kip spun his prisoner round again.

'Nothing,' he reported curtly.

'Good.' Robertson didn't lower the pistol. 'No comments, no queries, Carrick? From you that's out of character.'

Carrick shrugged neutrally. 'With what's pointed at me who needs questions?'

'That's being reasonable,' mused Robertson. His sallow face hardened. 'More reasonable than a minute ago. Well, at least you'll get your wish and see the girl. Move – the end door, you open it. But don't try to be clever. She already has company.'

The machine-pistol's muzzle nudging, Carrick went along the corridor, opened the door Robertson indicated, and went through into a small bedroom. Then he stopped, feeling a mixed wave of anger and relief.

Mora was lying on top of the bed, clothes and hair dishevelled, a trickle of blood from a gashed lower lip already dried down one cheek. Making an awkward, lopsided attempt at a smile she tried to sit up. But the thin cord which lashed her wrists behind her back made it difficult.

'All right, Mora?' asked Carrick softly.

'Reasonable,' she replied ruefully but relatively unperturbed. 'I'm not too happy about the company.'

Lounging back in a chair beside her, a long-barrelled deer rifle in his hands, one of the garage mechanics gave a snigger which held little humour. The left side of his face bore a series of deep parallel scratch marks, the damage moderately recent.

'The honours were even,' said Robertson equably, following Carrick's gaze. 'The girl did well. Ask Martin why he's in that chair. He came close to losing his manhood and still imagines he's crippled for life.' His manner changed and he thumbed towards the door. 'But you're not, Martin. Outside – make sure he did come alone.'

'The mechanic rose painfully, leaning on the rifle, and hobbled out of the room.

Kip cleared his throat noisily. 'This one should be tied,' he suggested, 'or –' he paused hopefully – 'will we shoot him?'

'The hard-line approach – you're out of date, Kip.' Robertson shook his head. 'Tying will do for now.'

The man produced a length of the same, thin, strong cord, dragged Carrick's wrists together behind his back, and lashed them tightly. Watching, Robertson quietly asked, 'You're still sure about what you saw at the village?'

'Positive.' Kip gave the knots a final tug. 'His crew are scattered ashore, his senior officer has gone away.'

Robertson's heavy face shaped a measure of relief. 'Then we'll take it you're here in a freelance role, Carrick. Or we'll hope so, for your sake as well as our own.' He pocketed the pistol. 'Right, down beside her on the bed.'

The order was aided by a heavy shove from Kip. Carrick tumbled, rolled and found himself flat on the mattress with Mora's head inches away.

'Comfort and a pretty girl,' chuckled Robertson. 'You should thank me. Or haven't you had any ambitions about this kind of situation?'

Carrick managed a shrug. 'I hadn't reckoned on having my hands tied.'

Robertson chuckled again, sat on Mora's side of the bed, and patted her leg. She tried to kick him and he gave a mild grunt as he moved back a little.

'Two questions, Carrick,' he said suddenly. 'And I want the truth to both. Otherwise –' His hand shot out again, gripped Mora's foot, and twisted it till she gave a tight-lipped gasp of pain. 'Where has Commander Dobie gone and why?'

There was no sense in lying. Not when he had a strong feeling the man already knew. 'He went south, because of the radio signals. That's where they reckon you'll be picked up.'

'Where the man they're after will be picked up,' corrected Robertson sardonically. 'If your commander really suspected me he'd still be in Quinbegg, agreed?' He shook his head almost sadly. 'Do you know what he'll find down there? Nothing – except a trawler which will make a great deal of fuss to attract attention.'

'While you skip out the back door?'

'If you mean to the north, yes.' Robertson regarded him equably. 'We have another trawler, one which has been quietly working its way round into position.'

154

'And you're going to sail out to meet her?' Carrick drew himself up on his elbows and laughed mirthlessly. 'That toy sloop you've got wouldn't last ten minutes in the kind of sea that's running. Even a trawler's going to have a rough time.'

Robertson regarded him for some seconds in cold silence then shrugged fractionally. 'We all have to gamble sometime. And with what I have to deliver –' He stopped short.

'The photocopies?' encouraged Carrick. 'I thought all the best Soviet spies had micro-dot outfits hidden in their underwear.'

Scowling, Kip took one step across and brought the butt of the machine-pistol down hard on his unprotected stomach. The pain was excruciating, almost overwhelming, and left him sick and gasping for breath.

'Enough,' murmured Robertson. He sucked his thick lips. 'You should be more polite, Carrick. For instance, if you could examine the knots on your wrists you would find they were seaman's knots. Kip happens to be short for Kiprowski ... Lieutenant Kiprowski, Soviet Naval Intelligence. We constitute a special service cell and fortunately for you I happen to be at least temporarily in command. Unusual, as I am the only one who is at least British by birth.'

A warning growl from his companion made no impression. Robertson waved a deprecating hand. 'It doesn't matter now, Kip. Even if we disposed of these two the operation is finished.'

'Including the Quinbegg Trench,' managed Carrick painfully. It got home. He saw twin patches of colour flare in Robertson's sallow cheeks and nodded. 'We're going to make it a "No Parking" area – particularly for non-resident submarines.'

Kip swore hoarsely. Robertson contented himself with a sigh. 'So Captain Jeffrey did make a report?'

'No. But he started us thinking.'

'After you killed him,' added Mora bitterly.

'Part of a gamble, an unfortunate necessity.' Robertson shrugged indifferently. 'The real credit belongs to Kip. He planted the charge. But afterwards – yes, matters did get a little out of control.'

'Meaning Leslie?' queried Carrick.

'Our stranger bearing gifts – the kind of gift we never dreamed existed,' mused Robertson. He smiled composedly. 'Don't worry about the Trench, Carrick. After tonight you will have no further visitors – not there, at any rate. And while I take the seafire data my colleagues will disperse. Our people are very good at contingency planning.'

There was a tap on the door. It opened and the mechanic looked in. His overalls were heavily flecked with rain and he was shivering.

'Well, Martin?' asked Robertson confidently. 'All clear?'

'Yes. But the weather –' The man shook his head expressively. 'It will be bad out there.'

'And better for us that way.' Robertson rose to his feet. 'Stay with these two. Kip will keep an eye on things outside and I've – well, a few things to arrange.'

'Going to try Eleanor again?' asked Mora, wriggling round to face him. 'What's the contingency planning for unco-operative wives?'

'She can come or she can stay,' said Robertson, his manner chilling several degrees.

'Mr Robertson has a problem, Webb,' said Mora unsympathetically. 'His wife doesn't like the way he paid the grocery bills . . . or how she found out, when he stuck a gun in my ear and made her answer the telephone.'

Robertson glared at her. 'The choice will still be her own.'

156

'I'd stay on dry land,' murmured Carrick, his stomach still aching. 'She'd be safer there – in more ways than one.'

Beside him Kip grunted and raised the machine-pistol again. But Robertson stopped him with a shake of his head. 'Carrick, my wife apart we plan most things carefully. For instance –' he smiled acidly – 'the radio transmitter your people are trying so hard to find. Would you like to know where it is?'

Carrick nodded resignedly.

'In the ambulance,' said Robertson cheerfully. 'Under the main platform, in one of the lockers. Right now our friend Vass, almost as good a mechanic as Martin here but a better radio operator, should be sending one last signal from our pretended base to the south. And when he is finished he will drive on again. Few people will stop an ambulance, fewer search it. And this one, after all, carries the body of Peter Leslie.' The smile widened. 'A nice touch, eh?'

Chuckling, he followed Kip from the room and the door closed.

Chapter Eight

The cord round his wrists was tight and unyielding, the knots as good as Robertson had forecast. Lying back on the bed, Webb Carrick stared at the plain ceiling above. Barging in the way he'd done had paid some dividends, forced Robertson out into the open – and there was always Eleanor Robertson as an unknown quantity in the background.

But with hindsight now he'd maybe have played it differently. As things stood the main picture certainly favoured the garage owner and his men. Commander Dobie's entire effort was being concentrated miles away, the *Clavella* was tied up and useless, only Sergeant MacKenzie remained. And he'd told the county policeman to wait for an hour.

If Harvey Robertson could handle that sailboat through the gathering gale and rendezvous with the second trawler ... he cursed at the thought. Once the trawler was outside territorial waters she could whistle up a Soviet escort. If there wasn't one already waiting.

From that moment on, short of an international incident, the seafire data was as good as in Moscow.

He turned on his side. Over near the door, slouched in a chair with the deer rifle across his knees, the man Martin reached into the pocket of his mechanic's overalls, took out cigarettes and matches, and lit one.

'Mora –' Carrick made no attempt to lower his voice – 'how did they get you anyway?'

'I wish I knew.' Easing round, she gave a sudden warning frown. 'Everything was fine till I tried to leave. Then they grabbed me.'

'No talking.' Tucking the deer rifle under one arm, the scratches on his face dark, swollen ridges, Martin got up painfully and limped over. He glared down at Mora. 'Particularly from you, you bitch. If I get any kind of vote on deciding what happens to you –' He stopped, grinned icily and left the rest of the threat hanging while he brought the glowing end of his cigarette till it almost made contact with the base of her throat.

Mora stared past him, her eyes fixed on the ceiling, her face pale. But suddenly the man grinned again and stuck the cigarette back in his mouth.

'Now shut up, both of you,' he warned, and headed back to his chair. Settled in it, he stroked his fingers over the barrel of the rifle, relaxed but watchful. After a minute he stirred again. 'Like to know who tipped us off about the girl, Carrick?'

'Enjoy yourself,' invited Carrick wearily.

'It was Robertson's wife.' The man saw his disbelief and found it amusing. 'She worried about the girl going out on her own this morning so went after her – and saw you meet. That didn't please her. The way she saw it, the lady still had boyfriend number one lying on a slab and had no business getting involved with a replacement. That's what she told Robertson when he got home.'

'Only he saw it differently,' mused Carrick.

'A whole lot differently.' The man winked then sighted casually along the rifle in Mora's direction. 'So he gave me the job of watching her as soon as I got out here. And I happened to see her slipping into the boathouse, then checked after she'd gone.' He tutted a mock disapproval. 'She'd cut through the spark plug leads on the outboard motor. But they're fixed now.'

'I heard Robertson telling Kip the boat was ready,' said Mora disappointedly. 'Sorry, Webb. It – well, it seemed a good idea just before I left. I didn't think they knew.'

'We know about most things,' declared Martin confidently. 'Now shut up like I said. The first one to talk gets gagged – that's a promise.'

They lay silent for a spell, listening to the rising wind and the occasional patter of rain against the window. Their guard lit another cigarette from the stub of the first and was halfway through it when the room door swung open and Kip looked in.

'Bring them through,' he ordered.

Shoved to their feet, the deer rifle jabbing them on, they were led to the big front room where, only twenty-four hours earlier, Robertson had entertained them as guests. But this time the scene was very different. Face flushed, eyes red-rimmed as if she'd been crying, Eleanor Robertson sat alone on a couch. All the curtains had been closed except for one window which faced towards the sea and Robertson stood there, frowning out at the heavy, dusking sky. Here, at the front of the house, the sound of wind and sea blended together in threatening chorus and the window glass shivered as one blast fiercer than the rest butted against it.

Robertson turned, ignored his wife, and addressed Carrick.

'You might as well know what's going to happen,' he said neutrally. 'As soon as it's dark enough, say another fifteen minutes, I'm taking the *Anna* out. Once I've got clear you'll be ferried to the hog-back rock and left there. Afterwards –' he shrugged – 'well, by the time you're found we'll be far away. All of us.'

'Including your wife?' asked Carrick.

Robertson pursed his lips. 'She prefers to stay. Her own choice.'

Eleanor Robertson looked up from the couch and nodded. 'I'll be with you and Mora,' she said quietly.

'She'll let them loose,' protested Martin from the background. 'Look, I –'

'You'll do what you're told.' Robertson glared him down. 'That includes tying her like they are. She already knows it.'

'That must be what's meant by "love, honour and obey",' mused Carrick.

Wordlessly, Robertson gave him a heavy back-hand cuff across the mouth. The blow stung but what mattered more was the look in the man's eyes. In that moment Carrick knew for sure. Though Harvey Robertson might never admit it, more than his pride had been hurt by the fact his wife wouldn't go with him.

Robertson turned away, crossed the room, poured himself a drink, swallowed it at a gulp, then glanced at his watch. 'I'll get ready now. Keep an eye on them – and outside too, just in case.'

Once he'd left, Kip took over. Under the machine-pistol's threat Carrick and Mora joined Eleanor Robertson on the couch. Then, satisfied for the moment, he beckoned Martin to join him. They moved back to the window, talking quietly, almost ignoring their prisoners.

'Mr Carrick –' the woman's voice was little more than a murmur – 'I'm sorry. I – well, I tried to warn you. Mora said –'

'I know,' he said softly. 'I understood. That's why I came.'

'Alone?' Her face was puzzled.

'There were reasons,' he whispered back. For a moment he was tempted to tell her there was still

161

a chance, that a lot depended on Sergeant MacKenzie. But she was still Robertson's wife, whatever her choice had been. 'Thanks for trying, anyway.'

'At least we look like getting out of this in one piece,' murmured Mora from his other side.

He nodded but wondered just what would happen after Robertson had gone.

It was grey dusk outside when Harvey Robertson returned. He'd changed his tweed suit for a heavy wool sweater and dark blue slacks, the legs tucked into a pair of cut-down rubber sea-boots. Over one arm he carried a waterproof jacket, and a canvas satchel was slung from his shoulder.

'Right,' he said, patting the satchel significantly. 'That's everything.' Coming nearer, he looked down at his wife. 'It still isn't too late to change your mind.'

She shook her head. Shrugging slightly, poker-faced, Robertson swung round. 'Let's go, Kip,' he said shortly. 'You know what to do afterwards.'

Kip nodded and followed him from the room.

They watched the next stage from the window, Martin in the background but too equally absorbed to object.

Heads bowed against the wind, Robertson and Kip left the house, trudged down to the beach, and launched a small dinghy which had been drawn up on the shingle. Kip at the oars, it bobbed the short distance out to the *Anna*, stayed there just long enough for Robertson to clamber aboard, then turned back towards the shore.

Little more than a dark shape in the failing light, Robertson moved around in the sailing boat's cockpit for a couple of minutes. Then, above the noise of the storm, they heard the short cough of the outboard motor starting. He appeared on deck again briefly, scrambling towards the bow to slip the mooring rope. That done, he returned to the cockpit and a cream of water gathered at the *Anna*'s stern as the outboard's propeller began churning. Mast still bare, riding easily over the swell, she began threading along the channel towards the open sea – where a boiling cross-pattern of waves marked the end of shelter.

Fascinated by the challenge, all that was at stake momentarily forgotten, Carrick found himself counting down the seconds to the moment when Robertson had to make his next move.

Suddenly it came. Quivering and shaking, the tight canvas of a close-reefed mainsail went up and was followed immediately by a tiny storm jib. An instant later the sloop's bow knifed into the lumping barrier of waves and simultaneously met the full force of the wind. Carrick winced as the little hull bucked and heaved, almost heard the snap of her canvas as the man brought her helm round and she went heeling over, the combined effort of outboard and sails fighting to clear the turmoil.

A heavy sea smashed against her, obscuring everything in a blanket of spray. He heard Mora gasp. Then, as the spray cleared, he could see the sloop was through and bearing away, still heeled over and close-reaching but with the wind's force suddenly in her favour.

Another moment and the *Anna*'s sails had vanished behind the long bulk of the hog-back rock.

'The show is over,' said Martin abruptly, some of the tension ebbing from his voice. 'Back where you came from.'

They obeyed. Tears were visible in Eleanor Robertson's eyes. Glancing at Mora, feeling suddenly helpless, Webb Carrick knew the bitter reality of defeat.

* * *

Though it probably wasn't much more than ten minutes it seemed a long time before Kip returned. He came into the room windswept and rainsoaked but with a broad grin on his normally surly face.

'He's clear,' he confirmed briskly, the machine-pistol held casually. 'It's bad out there, worse than I expected. But he should make it, Martin. I watched from the cliff till he settled on course.'

'Then it's our turn.' Martin licked his lips. 'Now?'

'The sooner the better.' Crossing over, his companion inspected their prisoners one by one. 'Starting by taking these people on our little boat trip. Though I would deal with them differently.'

'Like you did with Peter Leslie?' asked Carrick bluntly.

Kip's expression changed and he shrugged. 'Perhaps. That was simple enough. As for now – well, we might have been spared the trouble as far as you are concerned if Martin's rifle had been more on target last night.'

Martin coloured. 'It was a dark night and the range –'

'Was modest,' sneered Kip. He moved impatiently. 'Get them on their feet. We have our own schedule to meet.'

Martin hesitated. 'The woman was to be tied.'

'It can wait.' Kip grinned at him. 'Unless she makes you nervous.'

Outside the house the night had become a dark, blustering world filled with the steady pounding roar of breaking seas. Pushed into the lead, Carrick stumbled over the shingle with Martin immediately behind him. A few steps to the rear came Mora and Eleanor Robertson with Kip following.

'Why all the hurry?' asked Carrick over his shoulder, having to almost shout against the wind. 'Worried about something?'

164

His only answer was a curse. The deer rifle jabbed him low and viciously on the spine and he almost fell. It seemed wiser to stay quiet.

The dinghy had been drawn a little way out of the water close to some low rocks. As they neared it the rifle jabbed again.

'You first, into the bow,' ordered Martin. 'Up there, where we can –'

He didn't finish. A high-pitched shout of warning came from behind. Jerking round, Carrick saw dark shapes darting from the black shadow of the rocks and Kip frantically swinging the machine-pistol. But as it started to cough Eleanor Robertson's small, stout figure jumped at him, hands clawing. For a moment Kip struggled with her, then the machine-pistol stuttered again and she fell.

The running men had almost reached them. Initial shock over, Martin swore and started to bring his rifle into line – then went sprawling as Carrick shoulder-charged him. They went down together, falling hard on the pebbles while the rifle blasted skywards and clattered from Martin's grasp. Struggling round, straining against the cords on his wrists, Carrick saw the rifle now lying between them and the man scrabbling desperately to reach it.

Rolling on his back he brought both legs up together and lashed out. His heels smashed into Martin's ribs and sent him catapulting back, screaming with pain. As the man landed, two of the figures grabbed him. Sergeant MacKenzie's gruff voice rang out and handcuffs clicked.

But it wasn't over. Levering up on his knees, Carrick realized the machine-pistol had stopped firing – then saw why. Clapper Bell had Kip beside the dinghy, looming over him, massive hands gripping in a throat-squeezing stranglehold while he remorselessly hammered the man's head against the bow.

'Clapper –' Carrick shouted, then shouted again – 'stop it, Clapper. That's enough!'

Bell's hands relaxed their grip and Kip fell to the shingle without a sound. Cutting through the darkness a torch beam played briefly on blank, staring eyes and twisted features.

'God Almighty,' said Sergeant MacKenzie, visibly shaken. 'We don't need to worry about him. He's dead.' As the torch went out he produced a knife and sawed through Carrick's bonds. 'Will the phone at the house be working?'

'It should.' Carrick rubbed his wrists thankfully, looking round. Eleanor Robertson lay where she'd fallen, Mora and another figure bending over her.

'I'll try it. We need a doctor – for the others.' MacKenzie hurried off.

Clapper Bell was half-sitting, half-leaning on the side of the dinghy, breathing heavily. Leaving him, Carrick crossed over to the others. Eleanor Robertson was moaning faintly. Beside her, momentarily busy freeing Mora, he recognized Jim Haydock. The young research officer looked up, his face grave.

'The woman's pretty bad, sir. At least two bullets in the chest.' He glanced past Carrick, towards the rocks. 'And I don't know about Preacher –'

'He's here?' Carrick turned, surprised, and saw two more figures coming in. One was Matt Allison. He'd lost his spectacles somewhere and he had an arm supporting Preacher's thin frame.

'No worries sir,' reported Allison as he drew near. 'He's got a hole in his leg, that's all.'

'All?' Preacher's voice began to rise in protest then died away as he saw the rest.

'Webb –' gripping his sleeve, Mora brought him round again – 'she's trying to say something.'

He knelt beside Eleanor Robertson while Mora

gently pillowed the woman's head on her lap, sheltering her from the wind.

'Just take it easy,' he said softly, seeing her lips trying to shape words. 'We owe you a lot, Eleanor, so stay still. There's an ambulance on its way.'

She managed to nod but beckoned him nearer. 'Harvey –'

'What about him?' he asked quietly, glancing at Mora.

'I – I think I know where – where he's gone.' She stopped, taking a shallow rasping breath. 'I heard them talk. It was about – about a little island. Am – something. He said no one could land but it gave shelter. And there was something about birds –'

'What kind?' He bent closer, ignoring Mora's frown, a possibility shaping. 'Were they puffins?'

She nodded.

'Am Balg –' he said it softly, saw her nod – 'yes, I know it.'

Both puffins and guillemots bred on Am Balg, a rocky islet which rose precipitously from the sea about a mile off the mainland. No one ever landed there and it had a wide skirt of shoal rock. But it could give shelter in the gale, and it was only a handful of miles from Cape Wrath and the northern tip of mainland Britain.

Rising, rubbing his jaw uncertainly, he saw Preacher sitting nearby and went over. Clapper Bell was there too and greeted him sheepishly.

'I lost my temper a shade back there,' admitted the bo'sun. 'Sorry sir – it was seeing what happened.' He nodded over. 'How is she?'

'Bad.'

Bell nodded soberly then thumbed to where Allison stood guard over a hunched, gloomy Martin. 'Still, I'd say we timed it reasonably well.'

'That's an understatement. Sergeant MacKenzie didn't wait his hour?'

'A bit less than half o' it, then his feet got itchy,' admitted Bell. 'So he scraped us together and out we came – dumped the car about a mile back an' came along a wee cliff path Preacher knew about. That's when we almost walked into that character wi' the burp gun, and had to hang around an' guess what came next.'

Preacher grunted agreement, wrapping his black jacket tighter around him and shivering a little. 'Will the woman live, Carrick?'

'Maybe.' Carrick shrugged grimly. 'I hope so. We'll try moving her to the house, for a start. What about you?'

'My leg?' The gaunt face grimaced in the darkness as he patted the makeshift bandage just below one knee. 'I've done near as bad wi' a fish hook. It'll mend.' He sighed heavily. 'Like the Book says, man was born to trouble. Where's Robertson?'

'Making for Am Balg.' Carrick pursed his lips. 'And we can't stop him. Everything we've got is busy chasing a damned decoy to the south.'

Preacher snorted. 'What's wrong wi' your own ship, man?'

'No crew.'

'Says who?' demanded Clapper Bell indignantly. 'The mate said he'd have them aboard an' ready to sail. That's why he's not here.'

Hope flaring, Carrick stared at him. Then, just as quickly, the feeling died as he remembered Robertson's lead. The crashing waves seemed to rumble a dismal agreement.

'What time is it?' asked Preacher suddenly.

'About eight o'clock. Why?'

'Man, if you had to earn a living on this coast!' The deep voice held a sardonic edge. 'Tidal streams,

Carrick – if you don't know ask those bright-eyed boys. They'll understand.'

He called Allison and Haydock over. Backs to the wind, they listened soberly.

'Preacher's right,' agreed Haydock. 'You know how it goes, sir. The basics, I mean.'

Carrick nodded. They weren't talking about the undersea layers but the simple, ordinary surface streams of water common to any coast. They varied in strength and direction and behaviour, always hinged to the state of the tide. But they were always predictable.

'Well, if you took the *Clavella* west out of Quinbegg instead of north then about two miles out we could feel our way into a secondary surface stream – and it'll be flowing north right now.'

'You're sure?'

'Positive, sir. We've plotted the thing. It's thin, not much more than a ribbon of water, but we'd pick up an extra four knots riding with it – four knots at least, nearly all the way to Cape Wrath.'

'And an incomer like Robertson won't know about that,' murmured Preacher, easing his leg. 'Man, I'd try it.'

'With that leg you go nowhere.' Carrick calculated rapidly, seeing Sergeant MacKenzie crunching his way back from the house. Ten minutes' fast travel by car would get them back to the *Clavella*. And Robertson would have his own troubles out in that sea, would certainly be under drastically reduced sail.

They had a chance.

'The phone worked – the doctor's on his way,' said Sergeant MacKenzie as he arrived.

'Good.' He went over to Mora. 'I'm going after Robertson.'

'I heard.' She looked up at him soberly. Beside her

169

Eleanor Robertson lay very still but breathing more quietly. 'Can you make it?'

'Maybe.' He bent down and kissed her gently, avoiding the gash on her lip. 'You'll have Sergeant MacKenzie and Preacher. And I'll be back.'

He was on his way before she could answer.

Fourteen minutes later, at 20.05 as entered in the log, Her Majesty's fishery research vessel *Clavella* thrashed her way out of Quinbegg harbour with a full crew aboard. Some were unusually pale as she met the first open fury of the rising gale and began to pitch and barrel. But the solid green seas which crashed against her fo'c'sle then drained white from the scuppers provided a fast cure for hangovers.

In the wheelhouse, where the dull red glow of the night navigation lamps constituted the only light, Webb Carrick balanced against each lurching roll, heard the crash of loose fitments from below, and felt strangely satisfied. The lights of Quinbegg were already lost in the mixture of rain and spray and he was glad. The foam-streaked cauldron around was his real world – and for the first time this little ship was his own to command in the full sense of the word.

The *Clavella*'s tubby hull bucketed again, almost without warning. He saw the coxswain, a lean-faced AB with 'Mother and Maggie' tattooed on one bare, brawny forearm, automatically put down the helm to meet the shivering wall of water that momentarily towered above the port quarter. The wall broke viciously across the forepeak, more spray slashed against the wheelhouse glass, and the deck scuppers gushed white. Humming to himself, the coxswain deftly steadied the helm again, ready for the next.

Instinctively Carrick glanced at the compass card then at the clock above his head. The fast, steady thud of the Lister diesel at three hundred and fifty revolutions vibrated the matting beneath his feet. Jim

Haydock had called the tidal stream they were seeking a 'ribbon of water'. On the chart he'd been shown it looked more like a snake. But if they found it, if they slotted in and added the tidal stream's speed to their own, the result could make all the difference.

They needed much more than seat-of-the-pants guesswork on this kind of night. Which was where the radar set on the starboard side of the wheelhouse area came in. Haydock was there, crouching over the ghostly flicker of the viewing screen, working on fine scale and constantly checking the distance between ship and shore.

'How long?' asked Carrick.

'Soon, sir.' Haydock didn't look up.

'And where's Allison?'

'Still below – we've that other little job to finish, the one for Commander Dobie.' Haydock didn't elaborate.

Carrick grimaced at the reminder. Ever since they'd left harbour Sam Paxton had been practically barricaded in the radio room, supervising the feeding out of a long coded message which was going to cause consternation when it reached the fishery cruisers to the south and, simultaneously, their Chief Superintendent.

Another heavy hammer blow made the hull shudder. Below deck it brought a shattering clatter of broken crockery.

'She'll get worse afore she gets better, sir,' declared the coxswain philosophically, then frowned at the intrusion as the door on the lee side swung open and Clapper Bell came in. For a moment the gale's noise reached full volume then Bell slammed it out again and shook himself like a sheepdog, water cascading from his oilskins.

'That's us,' he reported, blinking the salt spray from his eyes. 'Deck lines rigged, all checked an' secure.'

He rubbed his hands cheerfully. 'If I'd been out there much longer I wouldn't know if I was punched or flamin' countersunk.'

'The barometer's still falling.' Carrick reckoned the wind had built to about Force Eight. He wondered grimly about Robertson, alone on that tiny sloop, taking at least as big a gamble in trying to get to his rendezvous before conditions reached their peak. He used the next roll to find the radar position. 'How long now?'

This time Haydock looked up, his thin face strained but confident. 'Almost there.'

Lifting the bridge phone, Carrick thumbed the engine-room button. Willie Dewar's gruff voice answered against the Lister's thundering background.

'It's coming up, Willie,' said Carrick crisply. 'Remember, we'll have this muck coming almost astern. But I want to keep as near full power as doesn't matter. Right?'

'I'll try.' Willie Dewar's metallic voice used a nine-letter word he treasured for moments of stress. 'But don't blame me if it tweaks the backside off us.'

'I won't. You'll get warning.' Grinning, Carrick hung up and waited.

'Now,' said Haydock after a minute. In the background, Clapper Bell braced himself against a stanchion.

'Bring her round gently.' Carrick rang standby on the telegraph. 'Starboard helm, steer oh-three-two.'

'Oh-three-two, sir,' repeated the coxswain, the wheel already turning.

The Clavella's head came round slowly but with immediate effect. As she came broadside on to the next sea the deck lurched, her starboard rail came down until it seemed almost parallel with the frenzied water, and the roll pendulum in the wheelhouse swung to an angle and stayed there for a long minute.

Then, gradually, as the m.f.v. still answered the helm's demand, the pendulum began to return.

The next sea broke aft. And the helmsman began humming again.

Though Haydock was confident, they had to wait for positive confirmation from the scanner and mechanical log. But it came – the *Clavella* was in the stream. The diesel was driving them on at twelve knots but in relation to the land they were travelling at over sixteen.

'But we could lose it again,' warned Haydock. 'Your first course correction should be in about three minutes.' Carrick nodded, listening to a brief alteration in the diesel's beat. It came again, a momentary cutdown in power in tune with a passing sea which sent the m.f.v. in a vicious fore-and-aft see-saw. Willie Dewar's engine-room team were avoiding any risk of over-racing, a risk present every time the stern left the water and the propeller rose clear.

The course correction came up, a tiny two degrees followed swiftly by another. His task complete, Sam Paxton returned from the radio room. Switched to the twenty mile scan, the radar tube showed a freckled, constantly varying pattern of wave movements. But on its fringe the scanner was picking up the hard outline of Am Balg.

'Port and starboard lookouts to position, Clapper,' said Carrick softly. 'All deck personnel to use safety lines. Searchlight team stand by.'

As Bell headed aft the wheelhouse telephone buzzed, Sam Paxton answered, frowned, and looked round.

'Radio room, skipper. *Marlin* is calling on the reserve frequency, personal for you.'

173

It had had to start sometime and the reserve frequency was well clear of normal fishery bands. Carrick drew a deep breath and reached for the handset. There was a pause, a whine of static, then a gruff, familiar throat clearing.

'You read me, mister?' came the barked demand.

'Loud and clear.' Carrick hid his amusement. Coming from *Marlin*, he might have known it would be Captain James Shannon. That explosive, moonfaced individual was probably chewing his beard with frustration and mentally cursing his absentee Chief Officer – plus a few other people.

'Good. Mother and your relatives are on the way but we'll be late. You understand?' Shannon didn't bother to find out. 'Anything positive on your radar so far?'

'Nothing yet. At present speed we're about fifty minutes south of the island.'

'Well, you've got a certain wee man in hysterics, though that won't do him any harm. But –' Shannon's voice faded then returned, faintly embarrassed – 'well, he's stuck on shore. And he says – he orders you've to keep the situation fluid till we arrive. Understood?'

'No,' said Carrick bluntly.

'Like hell you don't.' The static took over for a moment. Then Shannon came back again, his manner changed. 'Now I'm adding my own piece. Webb, till you rejoin my ship remember this. The *Clavella* is your command. Any commanding officer acts on his own discretion if a situation warrants it. Out.'

The relay ended. Slowly, Carrick replaced the handset.

'Anything important?' queried Sam Paxton suspiciously. 'From what you said, it sounded as if –'

'As if it was none of your damned business,' said Carrick curtly. He saw the mate flush and regretted it.

But Shannon had spelled matters out. Commander Dobie wanted him to act like a sheepdog till reinforcements arrived. If he went beyond that he was on his own, and whether things went right or wrong the can stopped at command level.

Meaning Chief Officer Webster Carrick.

The tidal stream didn't peter out until Am Balg had grown large on the radar's five mile scan. Which was exactly when Paxton, now hunched over the screen, gave a sudden grunt of interest.

'Better take a look, sir.'

Hopefully, Carrick joined him then tensed. A small blip had begun moving away from the sheltered eastern edge of the isle, travelling almost due north. He watched the screen closely, frowning as he tried to assess the vessel's speed, certain of its identity. To register so clearly under these conditions it had to be the trawler.

'Looks like Robertson made it,' mused Clapper Bell from the rear. 'They wouldn't shove off without him.'

Carrick nodded. 'And they'll have us pin-pointed on their screen by now.' From the blip's progress she was making about ten knots, which gave the *Clavella* a slight edge. But a little extra would help. 'Sam, ask Willie Dewar to coax up a few more revs. Coxswain, two points starboard.'

As the coxswain acknowledged and the mate reached for the wheelhouse phone the m.f.v. slid down a long, rolling, apparently endless swell then suddenly bellied out at the far side. Losing his footing, Clapper Bell staggered and swore.

'We'll take the east side of the island,' said Carrick for general benefit. 'I'll stay well clear of the shore. Clapper, as soon as we're under the lee get that searchlight earning its keep.'

Understanding, Bell nodded and turned to a voice pipe.

Minutes later they began to pass the black, surf-skirted silhouette of Am Balg's high cliffs. From its spray-lashed platform aft the big twenty-one inch searchlight flared to life, its lance-like beam wavering for a moment then sweeping round.

Halfway through its second sweep of the white-capped seas it hesitated then steadied. Simultaneously the port lookout shouted.

Snatching the wheelhouse glasses Carrick saw for himself. Forlorn, already well down by the head, Robertson's abandoned sailboat was being pounded in towards the rocks. One massive sea swept, curled, and almost turned her turtle. Then, as she struggled up again, that tiny storm jib still flapping, another wave smashed in.

He didn't want to watch the rest. After the ordeal she'd come through the *Anna* deserved a better fate. Lowering the glasses, he turned his mind back to what mattered.

'Searchlight off, please. Range to the trawler?'

'Four miles – we're closing!' A squeak of excitement filtered into Paxton's voice.

Inexplicably, Clapper Bell had vanished. But he was back before long, fingers round a slopping tea mug. He thrust it into Carrick's hands with a suspicion of a wink.

'While you've got the chance, sir.'

Carrick obediently sipped and tasted the liberal lacing of rum which had been added. He took a longer gulp, noticing the way the wind's whine through the rigging was becoming louder. Sheets of spray were drenching the *Clavella* from end to end as she battled on. Force Nine had arrived and Ten couldn't be far from its heels.

The gap was down to three miles when the telephone buzzed again. He snatched it impatiently with his free hand.

'Yes?'

'Radio room, skipper.' The operator sounded unusually puzzled. 'Thought I'd better tell you we're getting a strong local voice transmission. But I don't know what he's on about.'

'Is it Russian?'

'God knows,' said the operator bleakly. 'I'm from Belfast myself.'

Carrick put down the phone, knowing Paxton and Bell were watching and sensing the coxswain's ears were practically flapping.

'Our friend ahead seems to be shouting for help,' he said mildly. 'We've got him worried.'

At least it was nice to have company to that extent. He drained the last of the mug's contents, jammed it into a flag locker, and peered hopefully through the whirling circle of the clear-view into the murk ahead.

'She's slowing,' said Paxton unexpectedly after a spell. He studied the radar screen closely for a moment more and swallowed. 'Sir, she hasn't just slowed she – she's stopped. Or the next best thing.'

Carrick scrambled over, helped by a lurch of the deck. The blip was almost stationary, near enough to dead ahead. Mouth suddenly dry, he realized what it must mean.

'Keep watching.' While Paxton gaped he dived back to the telephone and jabbed the radio room button.

'Any more voice transmissions?'

'Yes, sir.' The operator's voice held a new tension. 'They're at it now – two of them, closer than before and nattering away thirteen to the dozen.'

Slamming the telephone down he snarled at the coxswain to hold his course and reached the screen again. The blip was less than a mile ahead, still

177

stationary but no longer alone. A second, larger blip was forming as he watched.

'Emergency full ahead.'

Pouncing on the telegraph Clapper Bell gave the imperative double ring signal on the indicator.

'Immediate signal to *Marlin*.' He thumbed the mate away from the screen while the diesel's pounding began to increase its tempo. 'Make "Trawler believed in rendezvous with submarine. Investigating." Add our position and time. Move, Sam.'

Paxton stood frozen for an instant then his mouth snapped shut and he jumped to obey while Carrick flicked the ship's alarm switch. As the m.f.v.'s klaxon began braying the coxswain gave a grunt.

'Lights ahead, sir.'

They were little more than pinpricks through the windborne spray but growing nearer by the moment. Carrick let the klaxon die and watched them, mentally urging the *Clavella* on.

'Signal on its way, sir.' Paxton turned from the wheelhouse telephone. 'But the engine room want to know –'

'Tell Willie Dewar to hold Emergency Full and to hell with the rest.' Carrick didn't look round, counting the seconds. At last, he drew a deep breath. 'Searchlight, Clapper.'

The bo'sun nodded, spoke into the voice tube, and the twenty-one inch flared to life again.

Almost immediately it settled on its target. Less than half a mile away, black-hulled, rust-encrusted, a hammer and sickle bold on its squat single stack, the Russian trawler was riding bow-on to the gale. There were oilskin-clad men on her deck, men who worked frantically, ignoring the seas breaking over them.

The searchlight shifted a fraction and pinned on the massive black sail of the submarine's conning tower. Through the glasses Carrick could pick out figures on her bridge, saw others struggling to stay upright on her exposed deck gratings. She was big, bigger even than he'd expected – one of the Soviet Navy's latest nuclear ships. A corner of his mind wondered just how many missile tubes she carried, how much destruction they might represent.

But what these men were doing mattered more.

'Extra light, Clapper.'

Two rocket flares soared from the *Clavella*, burst high above, and added their white magnesium glare to the scene. The submarine lay down-weather from the trawler and there was already a line across the hundred yard gap between them, a gap which was the absolute minimum in those crashing seas. And a small rubber life raft had just been launched from the trawler, one man aboard it.

Harvey Robertson was taking the seafire data on its last lap to certain safety. As Carrick watched, the men on the submarine's deck began hauling on the line and the raft began drifting down towards them . . . if drifting was the word for that slow, tossing, plunging progress, the raft rising and falling, disappearing entirely from view each time a wave trough sucked it down.

'Sir?' Paxton scratched nervously at his wisping beard, waiting.

Staring through the clear-view, his nails biting deep into the palms of his hands, Carrick watched the raft bob still nearer its target. Eleanor Robertson, Andy Jeffrey trapped in that submersible. Leslie . . . a whole lot more flashed through his mind in an instant of stomach-tightening decision.

'I'll take over.' He shouldered the coxswain aside, grabbed the wheel, spun it, watched the *Clavella*'s bow come round till it pointed at the submarine at a point just in front of that black, menacing sail, held it there, and knew his arms were quivering.

Someone – with surprise he realized it was the mate – had jerked the klaxon to life again, sounding Collision Stations. But he kept his attention rigidly ahead, seeing Robertson now more than halfway across, conscious of a sudden confusion on the submarine's bridge, of a moment's hesitation among the men on her deck before they started hauling again.

'Engine room maintain Emergency Full but stand by.' The words ripped from his mouth while his nerves wanted to scream their tension and the deck matting vibrated the diesel's torture.

Robertson had seen now, and knew. His face twisted briefly towards the approaching m.f.v. then turned away, working frantically with a tiny paddle.

Five hundred yards, the Russian trawler now large to starboard, her crew lining the rails in hypnotized fashion, her siren bellowing a mixture of protest and warning . . . and sweat beaded on Carrick's forehead.

'Auxiliary rudder drive stand by.' Every second, every yard, the chances of his gamble shrank, the final moment when he'd be forced to choose between complete commitment and defeated avoiding action came nearer. It had to be soon now. Someone had to give.

Suddenly the men were vanishing from the submarine's deck, her bridge was emptying till only one figure remained there. The figure raised a hand in a gesture which might have been anything. Despite the distance, Carrick knew who he had to be, knew his thoughts, knew the cost of the decision he'd taken.

And the submarine began diving while that last figure disappeared – leaving Harvey Robertson still thrashing the life raft nearer.

'Turning starboard.' The submarine's decks were awash, gone, the waves rapidly eating her fast-vanishing sail. 'Full auxiliary rudder drive. Emergency full astern –' Carrick croaked the order, already winding the wheel, watching the sail still sinking, gritting his teeth at the agonizingly slow way the *Clavella* answered while the telegraph jangled and the diesel shuddered and screamed its response. The m.f.v. heeled over, her whole being quivering, canting to starboard until her deck was taking whole water while an indescribable racket of crashing and breakages came from below.

But she had slowed, the sail had vanished, and they were turning short of the spot.

'Slow ahead.' He eased the helm, let the *Clavella* return gradually as the engine-room telegraph signalled, then clung weakly to the spokes for a moment. 'Take over, mister.'

'Aye aye, sir.' Sam Paxton was already at his elbow.

Surrendering the wheel, Carrick saw the searchlight still playing on the water but with a different purpose now.

'What happened to Robertson?' he asked hoarsely.

'We went over him,' said Clapper Bell with a fractional shrug, his face grim. 'He was in line when we dodged hittin' that sub.'

'We'll have to make sure.' Carrick said it wearily, looking round. They seemed suddenly, strangely alone. To the north the trawler was already heading away, her propeller churning a wake as if the devil was at her heels. That didn't worry him. He'd have taken a considerable bet on her crew being plain, ordinary fishermen who'd been caught up in the unexpected.

'Aye.' Clapper Bell paused and shook his head fervently, rank forgotten. 'Don't ever do that to me again! Do you know what would have happened if we'd thumped that sub?'

He could guess. If it had happened.

'She'd have gone home wi' a bit o' a dent as a souvenir,' spluttered Bell. 'But us hitting a thing that size? Hell, we'd have bounced off in wee bits!'

'Probably.' He felt weary now, his mind on that solitary figure who'd stared at him from the Russian's bridge. That man had known too, would have had to calculate the consequences of sinking an unarmed Government vessel inside its own territorial waters – then balance them against Robertson and the seafire data.

'Unless –' Clapper Bell swore softly to himself – 'unless you were at the old chicken game?'

Carrick wasn't sure himself.

Ten minutes later, guided in by the searchlight and working in still-worsening conditions, they brought the remains of Robertson's life raft aboard. And with it Robertson – or what the *Clavella*'s propeller had left, a sickening, mangled shape tangled into the parted line which had once been his link with safety.

Clapper Bell brought the canvas satchel to the wheelhouse. It was still dripping wet as he laid it on the matting.

'That what you wanted?' he asked.

Carrick nodded, then looked away. They were steering south-west, the barometer was beginning to rise a fraction – not the end of the storm but at least a lull, one that might last till they made Quinbegg. To port, Cape Wrath Light's beam was already visible, a high cliff-top pin-point in the heaving dark.

'Signal to *Marlin*,' he said quietly. 'No further assistance required, returning to harbour.'

Commander Dobie led the reception committee of police and security men who were waiting in a downpour of rain as the m.f.v. eased her battered hull alongside Quinbegg quay. Whatever he'd felt earlier he was in a jovial, back-slapping mood once aboard – particularly after he'd paid a visit to Haydock and Allison in the research area aft.

'You and I, Carrick,' he ordered crisply when he reappeared. 'Your cabin will do.'

They went there. As the door closed, Dobie rubbed his hands and looked around.

'Any of that bottle left?' he queried. 'I'd say a mild celebration is in order.'

'It smashed,' said Carrick apologetically. 'Sorry, sir – but we've got quite a breakage bill.'

'I know. Not to mention an engine that will need a complete stripping.' Dobie tutted a little. 'Dewar says you were – ah – a shade cruel in that direction. Not that I'm worried, of course.'

'You'll want this, sir.' Carrick crossed to the cabin's desk, opened a drawer, and handed over the canvas satchel. 'The dinoflagellate material.'

'Yes, of course.' Dobie hefted it happily. 'Though that little – ah – problem should settle itself now.'

'Sir?'

Dobie nodded, took out his cigarettes, and lit one. 'That idea I had, the one Haydock and Allison went to work on – it paid off.' He sent a studied jet of smoke towards the nearest porthole. 'Like to hear about it?'

Carrick waited, puzzled.

'Put simply, these dinoflagellates were different, fractionally altered. Now that could be several things – local sea temperatures, salinity, chemical factors. Or something else in addition, something we didn't know about at first.' Dobie pointed a triumphant forefinger. 'Those submarines in the Quinbegg Trench, Carrick. Nuclear powered – and with the finest safety precautions in the world, a factor I wouldn't particularly attribute to the Soviet Navy, you're always liable to some discharge of low-level nuclear – ah – pollution.'

'Radiation poisoning . . .' Carrick realized the rest and whistled softly.

'But diluted down till it was at an infinitely low level,' emphasized Dobie firmly then shrugged. 'Anyway, remember that even though the dinoflagellate bloom was out of its natural environment in terms of sea conditions, it was still capable of multiplying like fury. And if the radiation factor was enough to alter a few generations slightly . . .' He smiled with his lips. 'That's what I had them check, Carrick. Those water samples showed a fractional but positive radiation factor. Probably from your – ah – friend of tonight, if he's been resting around here lately.'

He sat back, the smile widening. 'That's your answer, Carrick. Local conditions plus a series of nuclear leakages – we'll double-check, of course. But these submarines won't be back. A polite warning to the Soviet Embassy will make sure of that much. As for the seafire bloom we're left with, I'd expect this storm to disperse it and kill most of it off. Local conditions will change enough in the next week or so to finish the rest and the fish population should be back to normal quickly enough.'

'Then it's over.'

'Once and for all,' agreed Dobie. 'Though we still keep our research material in cold storage, just in case.'

'And tonight's business?' Carrick eyed him suspiciously, sensing there was more to come.

'Well, the Robertson woman should live to wave many more banners and we got that damned radiohearse plus driver.' Dobie flicked the ash from his cigarette and grimaced. 'The rest of the matter will be settled quietly – the politicians are weaving something fairly delicate right now and don't want to be landed with a spy scandal. It's that kind of world.'

'Messy,' said Carrick grimly, listening to the rain lashing down outside.

'But the only one we've got,' mused Dobie. He rose to his feet. 'Well, *Clavella* looks like being stuck in harbour for the rest of this relief – the engine room think so, anyway. But you'll remain in command till you return to *Marlin*.'

'Yes, sir.' Carrick followed him to the door.

'Oh, and I nearly forgot.' Dobie winked. 'Preacher Noah claims you owe him a new pair of trousers, replacement for damage. And – ah – the Atholl girl has moved back to the Corrie Arms. She seems fairly anxious to see you.' The door opened, he paused with a twinkle. 'Want a lift in her direction?'

It was late, but he'd a feeling that wouldn't matter. And, suddenly, he seemed to have lost a lot of his tiredness.

'Well?' queried Dobie.

Carrick grinned, reached for his cap, and followed him.